SOULBLADE

The Genesis Gates: Stage One

PATTI LARSEN

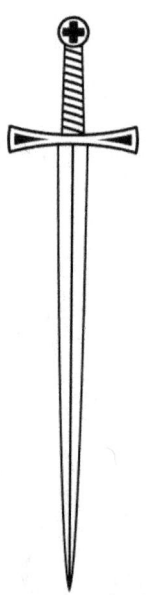

ISBN: 978988700151

ACKNOWLEDGMENTS

WITH MUCH THANKS TO Gary Gygax for making the first RPG Dungeons&Dragons an addiction for a nine-year-old girl. For my dad who brought that blue box with the dragon on the cover home in the first place. My sisters and cousins and friends for playing for hours and hours every weekend.

For my amazing betas, Christina Gaudet, Caron Prins and Kirstin Lund, who read everything I write and tell me the truth.

And, for Ladaar and Halflar Stonehand, for Lytron and all the members of my crew, thank you. Let's get together and play for old time's sake.

CHAPTER ONE

WHITE LIGHT BLINDS ME in a flare so bright I cry out. And then I'm tumbling forward, over and over, my body slammed to an abrupt halt. Groaning from the impact, I roll sideways in the brilliance, starting as a soft, female voice follows the musical ding of a bell.

"Selection complete. New stage activated. Soulblade scenario commencing."

Wait, what does that mean? My head spins, my mind aching but there's no time to ask, no moment to uncover where I am, what's happening to me. I'm moving again before I can understand, comprehend, even draw a breath.

The light whirls, sweeps across me like a river of rushing water, sends me diving forward again, darkness appearing at the end of the glow, hurtling toward me too fast. My hands rise of their own accord, shielding me as I exit the light and impact something hard, cold, damp and roll forward on one shoulder.

Instinct saves me from injury, though I groan from the landing, my skin wet from the back of my shirt where moisture seeps through. The light disappears, the world dark and moist, every breath heaving in my chest when I struggle to just draw air into my lungs.

My arm twinges, aches and I lift it to look, check for damage, whatever hurt causes the discomfort. But instead I see light yet clings to me, the same brightness I remember from a moment ago. Only not a tunnel-like fissure in the air any longer. The stark lines of letters and numbers etched into the flesh of my forearm flicker, the soft underside shivering from the flare of the glow. I stare at it, mouth filling with saliva as something visceral and emotional twinges, the need to throw up clenching my stomach. No memory, not really, not specific enough to call it that. Just the surety that this is my normal, whatever that means. Regardless of my reaction, like a desperate dog starving for scraps, I hang on as the light fades again, leaving me in dimness that makes it nearly impossible to read the inscription in my skin, a dark tattoo all that remains.

The groan that escapes me when I drop my arm to my chest has nothing to do with relief. It's torn from my dry throat when I release every muscle, collapsing utterly while my aching head throbs several times before easing off and giving me peace.

I should be terrified, shouldn't I? I have no idea where I am, why I'm here. Not a trace of what's come before the light and the woman's voice remains to me. And, as I let my beaten and shaken mind stretch outward into questioning, that's not about to change any time soon from the utter blankness I'm met with. Leaving me here, without a clue who I am.

I suffer one palpitation of my heart, a heavy, painful thud while it skips a beat in the face of fear. And then it plunges onward and I can breathe again, my aches vanishing, the dizzy incomprehension fading into the background when I force myself to sit up and look around.

This feels familiar, despite my lack of memory. Emerging from emptiness into wherever I've found myself might not be ideal, but at least I'm not incapacitated by indecision. There's an awareness embedded deep inside me, like it's part of me. An utter confidence that everything is as it should be. Comforting when terror would be a better fit.

In fact, not knowing is about as common a condition as I think I've ever known. How can someone become accustomed to knowing nothing? I shake off that question and instead inspect myself, my surroundings.

I'm in some kind of cell, enough flickering light, pale yellow and gold, likely from a source of fire, casting shadows and bits of illumination from somewhere past the heavy metal bars I'm facing. The walls and floor, the ceiling above me, all stone, are wet beneath my supporting hands. I wipe them on the thick weave of the pants I wear, boots to my knee tied tightly with leather thongs, my shirt tugged out of the belt around my narrow waist. Some kind of unbleached linen laced at the throat, sleeveless. I shiver as the damp settles in, rising slowly from the hard, wet floor, testing my body's strength and finding I'm in better shape than I expected.

The bars open into a hall beyond my cell—it must be a cell, with a low bench, a stinking pit for waste and little else—small and confining. The metal of my cage door comes away in rusting flakes on my hands when I grasp them, the lock a large and heavy flat plate, as pitted as the bars, but sturdy enough when I test the door with a firm tug.

"Good luck with that," a female voice laughs at me from across the corridor. She sounds young, lost to my vision in the darkness of her own confinement. I lean as far forward as I can, cheek pressed to the iron and look left, then right, as she goes on. "You made a spectacular entrance just now. I fully expected puking, but no luck. I guess that means I should be impressed?" Jaunty, her tone, carefree despite her captivity.

"I suppose," I say. From what I can see, the stone corridor extends in both directions, large torches mounted flush to the walls between cells dancing flame in the faintest movement of air. Left. That means the exit is left, doesn't it? How do I know how to sort that out if I can't remember anything?

I lean away and peer into the cell opposite me, but it's too dark to see anything. Instead, I look down at my arm again, examine the tattoo in the slightly better light I've gained at this angle.

Written across the top, I read: PLAYER WEBB-G. Webb. Is that my name? Player of what? Beneath it are six sets of letters in a row, with numbers corresponding: PH, ME, SP, EM and 13, 12, 09, 13 in turn. HW is next, 24 assigned to it. For some reason that number pleases me, but I can't figure out why, just an instinctual reaction. And, finally, BL with the letters FH. I touch the tattoo but it's flush with my skin and no longer aches. Without any context to offer clues, I drop my arm and let that curiosity go for now.

"Did your capture addle your brains?" She's having fun with her taunts, apparently. "You're not much of a talker, are you?"

"Maybe if you had something important to say," a gruff voice says beside me. From the next cell down? Male this time, like mine, only deep and graveled. "Meanwhile the rest of us get to listen to your obnoxious chatter and wish you were in reach."

"Poor dwarf," the girl's voice rises in pitch and irritation, more than likely on purpose. How long have they been down here? And how many more, exactly, considering he used the term, "rest of us?" "Am I bothering you so very much?"

The voice in the next cell grumbles something that sounds like a curse in another language, the intent apparent even if the literal translation isn't offered. My mind automatically tells me he's speaking a dwarfish dialect as if instinct is more important than memory. At this moment, I suppose it is. "Go choke on your slop," he finally grunts.

"Are you recovered sufficiently to test your lock?" That's from the other side of the girl across from me, forward on my right. I catch movement at last, someone drifting to the bars to peer out at me, her tall, slim form cast in the flickering light of the torch beside my cell. Her long, sweeping ears arch backward from her narrow face, eyes deep set from shadow, angular features and elongated limbs clearly elvish in origin. I don't question I know she's of another race than me—I'm human, I'm sure of that—nor that I recognize what she is. Long, pale hair hangs over one shoulder, wound in some kind of elaborate braid, thin hands rising to grasp her own bars.

"I have," I say, rattling the door to no avail as proof.

She sighs and nods, disappearing back into the darkness of her own cell. "As expected."

"Why you even bother," the grumbling voice of the dwarf on my left complains. "Elves and their optimism."

"She's not the only one who holds hope." The newest voice comes from my right as well, but beside me. So I'm flanked by a grouchy dwarf on the left and another male on my right, this one with a deep, rich tone that reminds me of something I can't put my finger on. Cultured, smooth, with practiced care of phrase and pronunciation, almost as if he's been trained as a singer or public speaker. He sounds large for some reason, like he's holding back volume and I wonder now with awoken curiosity who I've fallen into hard times with.

The final voice comes across the corridor and on the left, on the far side of the happy girl who spoke first. "We can't just sit here," she growls, coming to her bars much as the elf had. Another human, like me, only female and angry, lips in a gash of a line across her pale face. I make the connection we're divided by sex, female on one side, male on the other, when she speaks again. "His arrival changes nothing. We're still without a plan."

"You go ahead and plan away, mighty paladin." The cheeky girl across from me finally pokes her nose against the bars and I grin despite my predicament. A halfling, barely taller than my waist, furry feet padding silently on the stone, her own smile answering me in bright greeting, saucy wink tossed casually in my direction. "If you can think of something, I'm all ears." She giggles at that like it's funny, her own pointed like the elf, though without the sweeping elegance, more spring buds than fully formed leaf shapes.

The paladin woman sighs and meets my gaze, frustration written on her stern features. She's attractive enough, maybe in her mid-twenties, without the refinement of the elf. But her broad shoulders and large hands that grasp the bars before her tell me the halfling knows what she's talking about.

"You're all useless," she snaps before turning her back, leaning against the bars. The large dragon that's embroidered on her surcoat glares at me through the barrier like it blames me for the mess I'm in, the mess we all apparently share.

I'm about to apologize for not being the bearer of better news—heavily dosed with sarcasm since I'm as much a prisoner as they are—when a distant sound of metal grinding and the heavy thud of a door being shut catches my attention.

The sound of footfalls, again to the left in the same direction as the air flow, heavy and lacking any kind of stealth, silences the others. The paladin retreats, though it's the single fingertip to the lips from the halfling before she disappears into the depths of her cell that warns me I should do as they do and find a hiding place in the darkness.

Too late, I catch the approach of what has to be a guard, the torchlight reflecting from the faint green of his skin and catching the moisture of his bulging eyes just as he comes to a jingling halt before me. My mind instantly identifies his race with a kind of detached logic that makes me feel wobbly. Though, my otherwise empty history does nothing to defer the truth that strikes me.

Hobgoblins smell like sewers.

"New boy," it grunts, smacking its grossly thick lips, a large and bulbous nose flattened faintly off center in its pockmarked and scabby face. "Time for your lesson."

CHAPTER TWO

I KNOW INSTANTLY I'M in for trouble and back away from the bars, hands clenching at my sides as I prepare for the inevitable. The hobgoblin uses a large key on the lock to my cell, dropping it back into a pouch at its waist when it pushes open the door. I could tackle it, perhaps, and try a preemptive strike but it's faster than I expect and when I try to lunge for it when the door is still open it lashes out with a fist and strikes me in the ribs, doubling me over from pain and forcing air out of my lungs. Such an attempt has to be typical of all its prisoners and

I've just put myself in exactly the position it wanted me.

I clutch at my side, berating myself for my idiocy while my arm twitches. A quick glance down shows the number under HW glowing a moment before dropping to twenty-three. That double digit is tied to my health and wellness. How do I know what HW means? Doesn't matter right now, not while my ribs ache from the blow. Good enough to realize, though, the drop is a bad sign, I'm positive of it, but there's not much I can do to change that now.

No time to work out why I know what I know, nor even what to do next. Not when the guard lashes out for the second time in almost casual boredom, as if this is a chore it's grown accustomed to and would prefer someone else handled. One of its heavily booted feet strikes my knee with the unyielding toe reinforced with metal. I can't stop the scream that exits my already sore throat, landing hard on the ground and curling into a ball to try to protect myself while it kicks and stomps at me, grunting over me when it delivers the beating that is my lesson.

When it's done I'm aching all over, but I'm still intact enough I remain conscious as it backs off, wiping at a line of drool dangling from its thick lips, sweat beading on its sickly green skin.

"You give me trouble and I'll break you next time." Its thick accent makes it hard to decipher what it is saying, but I process enough I nod in agreement, staying where I am, as it turns, its rusting chainmail jingling as it exits my cell and locks the door behind it. I watch it go, waiting for silence before I uncoil from my fetal position and gingerly test myself for damage.

My HW has fallen to twenty-one, but rather than worry about that creeping descent I continued to examine myself in the low light.

"Our host didn't kill you, I take it?" Though clearly an effort at being chipper, all the good humor is gone from the halfling's voice.

"I'm here," I croak, unashamed of the previous cries that graveled my voice, knowing now the rest of them must have endured the same upon their arrival here. "I take it that's a regular occurrence?"

"Just a friendly reminder all hope has fled," the halfling says, singsong tone regaining some of her amusement. "That we should simply give up and accept our lot in life and that we'll never, ever escape or see the light of day, so on and so forth, ad nauseam."

"Shut up, won't you?" The dwarf sounds furious, voice vibrating. "I'm tired of your chatter."

"Come over here and tell me that," she shoots back, words edged in laughter.

I choose to ignore them, turning to lean with my back against the bars, chin on my chest a moment as I inhale, exhale the stale air, recovering as best I can by holding still. I finally open my eyes, the banter in the hall fallen quiet. There's an excellent likelihood I passed out just now and am only awakening again. So be it. Rest might be what I need. It's done nothing to return my memories, though, and while I'm hardly surprised I am disappointed.

I look up, sighing deeply past the aches tugging at my body with the depth of my breath, and realize I missed two important items in my cell.

The scaled and cracked water jug holds musty liquid but I gulp it anyway after a hasty test sniff, thankful for the moisture. I choke on the first swig, throat closing as if in protest of the flavor, but I force it down until my body accepts it. The dryness washed from my throat, I turn to item number two and the flat plate with the missing chunk from one side. Its molding bread might have been unappetizing in normal circumstances, but my stomach thanks me for the offering after I pick off the worst of the fuzzy green growth. There's sufficient food remaining I feel full enough, especially after drowning what I've eaten with the rest of the water. For a moment, my gut churns, debates the offering and I hold my breath, hands pressed to my middle, begging everything to stay where it is and not reemerge and waste what I've been given.

When my stomach finally flexes and relaxes again, I sag, head bowing once more, this time in relief. My arm tingles when I do, HW glowing faintly, rising to twenty-two. Food, water, maybe some further rest could restore me more? I have zero doubt that number connects directly to how I am feeling and my physical state of health.

I need to sleep, not pass out. Real sleep with the restorative benefits of that. More knowing without memory how I know, but I'm learning not to let that bother me. One thing is certain, if I'm going to recover further, I have to rest.

But when I moved to rise, to reach for the bench so I don't have to sleep on the floor, my hand slips over something cold and sharp that jingles faintly on the rock. I jerk back from it with a soft hiss, the sharp edge of it slicing my finger. I suck at the bead of blood that rises, peering down toward the stone floor and the single metal circle lying there. The shorn rim has cut me, severed link of chainmail discarded, I can only imagine, from the hobgoblin's armor when it delivered my recent lesson.

Heart pounding in hope, I lift the ring and examine it. The diameter of the metal seems decent enough, so much so that when I try to straighten it from its present shape it takes considerable effort. I grunt faintly at the task, cut finger oozing blood and making the job slippery, my thick fingers struggling to hold tight enough to bend the round into length. I finally win against the stubborn metal and, when I'm done, I hold a three inch piece of heavy gauge wire in my tired hands.

My knees protest the harsh firmness of the rock beneath them as I kneel immediately, all thought of rest vanished at the hope rising escape might be imminent. I examine the lock on my door as best I can from the far side. Its opening faces the corridor, my fingers exploring the edges of it, no access from my side kyboshing my plans to make this quick and easy.

Rustling across from me precedes the interest of the halfling who moves forward to watch when I slide one hand through the bars again and use my still oozing index finger to guide and insert the wire into the lock on the other side.

"You trained to do that?" She sounds excited, all sarcastic teasing gone.

I grunt at her instead of answering her silly question, focusing on the task at hand, unwilling to admit to myself I have no idea what I'm doing. My hope stirs this continuing knowing without memory might kick in and allow me to pick the lock. No such luck this time. And I realize I'm not going to get much further on my own when my arm tingles and the PH vibrates, turning faintly red. *Physical*, my mind whispers. Tied to my strength and skills, but also to my nimbleness of movement. In this case, I just don't have the number I need to succeed.

Frustration pings against my traitor memories and their selective information. Faint sweat beads on my upper lip when I refuse to quit. After a moment of trying to figure out what I'm doing, however, and a near loss when the wire slips in my bloody fingers—the halfling hissing her concern when I lunge and catch the metal length just in time—I finally give in, fingers aching from the awkward positioning and sink back on my heels to think.

"Toss it over here." The halfling sticks one skinny arm through the bars, her tiny fingers wriggling in eager anticipation. "Hey, are you listening? You might be a total useless klutz without a scrap of talent, but I can use that."

I hesitate, both from the insult and the need to think her demand over, bouncing the wire in my hand. "You can free yourself?"

She wrinkles her nose at me, grins. "Naturally," she says. "What's a rogue good for if I can't pick a simple lock? And you, my friend, have the perfect tool for my liberation at your disposal." She glances to her right, my left, down the corridor toward the exit where the guard has disappeared. "Hurry up, then, handsome, and make a choice." She bats her eyelashes at me. "You want out too, don't you?"

More rustling, interest raised as the others come to their bars. "Don't trust her," the dwarf says as the elf leans close to her door and peers sideways toward the halfling's extended arm.

"Don't listen to him," the tiny thief says while the others remain oddly silent. Does that mean no one trusts the adorable halfling who looks like an innocent child? An excellent thing to know. "Give it." She wriggles her fingers again, anxious excitement on her face, round cheeks pink with it. "What are you waiting for?"

"How do I know you're not going to just run off and leave me behind?" I have already made my choice, though, despite my hesitation. I can't use the wire to pick my lock, that is obvious. And no one else has spoken up, either to support her or to make the same request—demand—she's making. Besides, she's right across from me and the easiest to reach. A simple toss could mean my liberation. So giving it to her, the most logical person to get the job done, is the best decision. And yet, I can't help but prod her for a word of faith.

She sighs with the kind of dramatic annoyance that makes me smile wider. "No promises," she quips. "I am a rogue, after all. Still, I'm being forthcoming about that fact. And there happens to be honor among my kind from time to time."

"Between your kind," I say. "What does that mean for the rest of us?"

She snorts. "Clever, I'll give you that." She finally shrugs, acting casual, leaning against the bars with her arms crossed over her chest. "Tell you what. You give me what I need, fighter boy, and I'll do what I can to do the same for you."

"She only needs you to fight for her so she can escape," the dwarf grumbles.

"Sounds about right," I say and toss the wire toward her without further conversation. "Catch!"

CHAPTER THREE

SHE NABS THE STRAIGHTENED link in midair, snatching it with ease before jamming it into her lock with the kind of confidence that assures me I made the right choice. Humming softly to herself, her face twisted into a tiny frown, tongue peeking out between her lips, she wriggles the length of metal like she can see through her door until something clicks a moment later. With a huge sigh of satisfaction, she firmly pushes her door open, though I wince at the creaking groan of it and even the cocky halfling freezes, tense and wary, until silence lingers long enough it's apparent no one is coming to investigate the sound of her escape.

She prances out into the corridor, little body limber and apparently none the worse for wear. Either it's been some time since her own lesson with the hobgoblin or she's much quicker to bounce back than I am. She pauses to bow to me with the wire still firmly in her grasp. She wiggles it at me before blowing me a kiss. "Good deed done," she says before sliding it into my lock and freeing me a moment later.

I emerge from my cell more carefully than she exited hers, easing the door open to minimize the sound of tortured metal on metal. Mine, apparently, has seen some kind of lubrication recently because it's not nearly as noisy as hers regardless of my caution. She stares up at me when I'm fully free, hands on her hips, dark brown topknot bouncing as she taps one foot on the floor, giant grin on her face. I look up and to the left and right, down the long, darkening hallway in both directions. One end, the exit from the hobgoblin's recent movements, has torches at intervals, a door visible in the distance. The other stretches out into black. No other prisoners in this cell block, then?

"You're not seriously going to leave us behind?" The paladin stands at her door, her face set in fury, hands clenched on her bars so tight her knuckles look like living things crawling under her skin. "Are you?"

"Maybe," the halfling winks up at me, cockiness her normal, I can only guess. "What's in it for us?"

"Your life, when I get my hands on you." The dwarf raises his voice, too loud for my liking. I wince and pivot to shush him with a gesture while I nudge the halfling toward the paladin.

She gapes at me, little face falling, big eyes wide, eyebrows arching into her shorn line of dark bangs. "You're not serious."

"Neither are you," I say, knowing it's true and no longer amused by her teasing. Cute has turned to a push too far. "Now stop being bratty and hurry up. Before the guard comes back."

She grumbles, shoots me a peevish look, but I know she's just doing it for show because she's light on her feet and cheerful when she finally bounces away and begins opening cell doors, whistling faintly. My arm vibrates and I look down to see the letters FH under the BL glow a moment in white. *Faithful hero*, my beliefs and the code I live by. How odd and yet comforting to have that from my reluctant mind. I look up from my embed—I have a name for it now, for the tattoo, though what an embed is I have no idea—to find the elf was the halfling's first pick and has joined me, her height a match to mine though she's willowy and thinner boned. The paladin is next, her long, red hair bound at the base of her skull, crimson surcoat torn, one sleeve of her long shirt ripped. I turn as the halfling opens the door on my right, and almost cry out before I catch that instinctive warning more for myself than the others and swallow it.

A troll steps out into the corridor, his massive shoulders brushing the ceiling, head bowed to keep him from hitting it on the rock. He has to turn partially sideways to stand next to us, large hands curved into soft fists, knuckles almost touching the floor. His jaw juts forward, two tusks carved with strange symbols curving upward over his thick upper lip, and matching horns twine around his large, leaf shaped ears, the same etchings visible in the pale ivory. But despite his massiveness and the bulking musculature, the hulking monstrosity of his pale gray skin and the instinctual fear I feel at facing one of his kind, there's a gentleness in his deep, blue eyes, large and sunken into his craggy face, that makes me pause and question my gut reaction.

"Thank you," he says in that same mellow voice, nodding to me, tone careful, words as precise as ever. "I know I don't always instill confidence when I first meet other races, completely understandable considering our history of not playing nice with others." He could say that again. Troll wars. I've fought his race before, I'm positive of it. Though there was a horse under me at the time, right? And wasn't the troll I fought three or four times the size of this still impressive if unthreatening fellow? A memory, though inaccessible beyond the initial impression, still something I take as a good sign of the possibility of more recovery as the looming figure goes on. "And without my normal accoutrements you could mistake me for a wild troll."

"Which you're not," I say.

"Druid, second class," he says. "Vosh Troljedur, at your service."

"If we could save the introductions for later," the dwarf snaps, now free and glaring at the halfling who thumbs her little nose at him. He looks up at me, rolls his dark eyes, heavy brown beard unkempt and bristling over the dirty front of his pale brown tunic.

"Agreed." The paladin looks past me and then turns to the exit. "We need to check the other cells for possible weapons."

"As if our hobgoblin host would leave anything valuable behind," the elf murmurs, but she sounds less judging and more practical about it. And I agree with her. Still, if there is a chance, we can't turn it up.

"It's just us," the halfling says but she's already looking herself, peeking inside each closed and barred doorway while the rest of us ease forward, letting her lead. It feels wrong to me for her to take the front, and yet that configuration makes sense so I shove down my protective surge and stay close enough I can guard her from harm if need be. Though what I'm going to use to do the guarding with is beyond me.

I need to figure out how to connect what I instinctively know and what I don't remember with my reality before it gets me into too much trouble.

I eye one of the torches in its bracket as I duck past, the flames welcome warmth near my face, dispelling the damp briefly, brave, dancing fire a beacon in this inhospitable place. Could be used as a weapon in a pinch, a club of ash and sparks better than nothing. I'd much rather a sword or dagger at this point, but beggars can't be choosers.

"Here." I join the halfling to find a cell with an occupant stretched out on the narrow bench carved from the wall. No movement, no breath and I'm positive before she even reaches out to pull the cloth from the face what she'll find. A grinning skull greets her efforts, making her squeak faintly and jump, though she releases a nervous laugh and smiles at me over her shoulder like she's honestly having the time of her life.

"Better him than us, yes?"

I shrug, ease past her, poking at the remains, though it's just rags and bones and nothing else of interest or use from what I can see. I do feel vaguely guilty over disturbing the dead, but he's not here to argue with my investigation so I retreat and silently wish him well as I exit into the corridor.

"Nothing then?" The elf doesn't seem surprised, the paladin grim about it.

"I'd say that's a no from what we've seen so far," I say. "And that's good enough for me." I gesture at the exit door, now closer to us. Enough that I'm nervous we could have a visitor at any moment, an unexpected return of our hobgoblin jailer. While some of us could duck into a cell and hide if the guard came back, the troll is going to have difficulty maneuvering that fast and his exposure means we're all at risk. Though the thought does cross my mind a single hobgoblin will be in for a very bad time if he chooses to appear just now.

Enough the idea of his death by crushing force under the troll's large foot makes me grin at the imagined sound of his final splat.

"Here, handsome." The halfling presses something into my hand and I look down to find she's given me a sharpened piece of bone. I almost shudder from it, until my fingers close around it like they know exactly what to do with it even if my sensibilities are disgusted. "Don't ever say Blossom Riverbend doesn't look after her friends."

"Are we friends?" I can't help smiling at her.

She shrugs. "If you're nice to me."

I should be horrified to hold someone's remains in my hand and anticipate using it as a weapon, but it makes me feel more secure so I shrug off any reticence and gesture to the exit.

"Should be" seems to be a term I'm going to have to discard if I'm planning to escape this place.

Instead, I focus on here and now and our next step and am rewarded with a confident surge of my own good humor. "Shall we see what's on the other side of that door?"

They don't answer, they don't have to. Because what's on the other side of the door chooses that exact moment to show its ugly face. The hobgoblin doesn't notice us at first, hands full of bucket handles, two in each grubby fist, eyes down on the floor as it turns and kicks the door shut behind it. When it spins around again, it finally looks up. Freezes. Gapes. For a comically long time, it feels like, as if waiting for something to happen, for things to revert to normal.

Not that it matters what the hobgoblin is doing, ultimately. In fact, it can stare as long as it wants, for all the good it will do. I'm already running toward it on feet that move of their own accord, body called to battle like my mind isn't connected to it. The bone knife feels right, gripped tightly in my hand, the embed in my arm tingling and glowing red when I close the distance between me and my target and pounce.

CHAPTER FOUR

IT'S NOT MUCH OF a fight in the end, though I'm a bit disgusted by the clumsiness of my own actions. I would blame the fact my brain and body aren't really working as one, but the truth of it is, killing something—even as wretched a thing as a hobgoblin—is messy, horrible business.

I run flat out toward the guard while he shakes himself free of his frozen state at the last instant, leaping while he struggles to drop the buckets, the handles catching on the barbs growing from the filthy flesh of his wrists. He manages to turn sideways while I'm in midair and partially evade me, but I crash into him, the impact inevitable from the moment I launch from the ground, and take him down with my weight as my first weapon, landing on top of him with the bone knife raised before I can think.

I plunge it into his neck, watching as if from a distance the sharp end puncturing green, glistening blubber at the base of his throat. The gurgling of his breath escapes his thick lips, turning to a bubbling sound easing around a sigh, blood pooling out of the hole I made when I jerk the knife free, pooling up into his mouth and spilling over. I drive the bone point deep into a new place, severing several important connections that sustain what's left of his life and feel him twitch under me as he dies quickly. With a last twitch he half sits upright, spurting a messy gout up and over my hand, splashing my front with crimson before he rattles deep in the back of his throat and collapses.

Over in between the pulse of one heartbeat and the next, his last. So fast I inhale and realize I failed to do so recently, the breath jagged and filling my aching lungs with much needed air.

There's a stunned silence inside my mind, though my body seems utterly at ease wiping someone else's blood from the back of my hand onto the crusted hem of the hobgoblin's tunic just below his chain shirt.

My arm aches but in a good way as the red glow of the embed fades to white and then back to black. I rise and step away from the body, smearing away a few droplets of blood I feel drying on my face, the others joining me. I stand there, panting and knowing this could have gone badly if Blossom's gift hadn't been in my hand while said halfling slips past me and begins an efficient and cheerful search of the body.

"Well done," the paladin says, looking me up and down as if only realizing now she's underestimated me.

I nod back, aware I've been underestimating myself, so I can hardly fault her for it. "Can't just be him guarding us," I say, accepting my lack of horror at my willingness to kill as one more thing I just need to get used to. For some reason, as real and tangible as this is, I feel distant, like none of it matters, not really. As though what

I've just done isn't the first time nor will it be the last and only my goal has importance.

What goal is that, though?

"He's the only one we ever see." The troll peers over my shoulder, Vosh sounding curious and calm, drawing me back from the confused spinning in my mind. "But you're likely right."

Blossom steps away from the dead hobgoblin, grinning up at me, a knife now strapped to her belt, her shirt tucked firmly into the leather. Stolen from the guard, both items, and gleefully in her control.

"Hand that over." The dwarf makes a grab for her past me but she skitters aside, leaping the body and putting the sprawling dead hobgoblin between her and him. A quick kick at a bucket sends slop that must have been meant for our next meal pouring out onto the stone floor in an oozing mess.

"Mine," she snaps.

"Actually," the elf says in her soft, musical voice, "I believe it's for our friend here to lay claim." She gestures gracefully to me. "Fair's fair, Blossom."

The halfling pouts at the elf then grins at me, batting her lashes once more. "Friends, right?"

I laugh, I can't help myself. "If it weren't for the knife you made me," I say, "this might have ended differently. So the dagger is yours. My gift to you. Friend."

Blossom curtsies. "My hero," she says before flashing a *so there* smile to the others and turns to the exit while the dwarf glares like I just stabbed him in the back. I have a feeling their bickering is going to get on my nerves about as much as it amuses me at the moment, though there's not much I can do about it either way. I have a feeling we're going to be together for a while.

I help the paladin stuff our former guard in one of the cells, dragging his surprisingly heavy body across the stone floor. She was nice enough to leave the feet to me, though I slip and skid over the trail of blood his gaping neck wounds shed on the floor beneath him so maybe she made the right choice taking his arms after all. There's no way to hide the blood trail, and anyone who looks down will realize there's been a fight and someone's lost enough blood they can't have survived the battle. Still, we can make it harder for the hobgoblin's fellow guards to locate its body and, knowing how they lack in a level of intelligence most other races enjoy, such a search might slow them down enough to let us escape.

That is, if we can even make it past them on the other side of that exit door. Or even open said door. I'm leaving that part of the job to the halfling Blossom.

When the paladin lets go of her end deep in the cell we chose for its resting place, I briefly consider a bit of my own body picking. I hesitate before helping myself to the rusting chainmail while my companion shakes her head when I offer it to her first.

"I'll wait until something less fragrant comes along." She crosses her arms over her chest as I don the armor, the weight of the metal slithering over my shoulders when I slip into the open side. Our guard has clearly stolen this from someone else because the sides gape, tied shut with a series of small leather straps. At least I can get a reasonable approximation of a fit, though I think it must have belonged to someone a lot smaller than me. Still, I feel much more protected despite the stink of the rust and the clinging odor of hobgoblin. And when my arm vibrates and I look at my embed, the PH shivers, the number beneath increasing from thirteen to fourteen. I'll take it.

I follow the paladin out into the corridor again, closing the door behind the dead guard. The others remain at the exit, arguing quietly, while I shake my head and hurry to join them. Surely they have it open by now? But no, it remains firmly closed. The troll, dwarf, elf and halfling make no move to leave, so obviously either they're fighting over who goes first or there's a problem opening the way. It's clear when I look around Vosh's bulk they're having difficulty getting the door to do what it's meant to do and I push my way through to get a look at what the holdup is.

CHAPTER FIVE

I GET MY ANSWER before I even ask, the paladin joining me in the shadow of the troll.

"It's some kind of spell." The dwarf rubs his hands together, though he looks grim, not excited. "I can't seem to identify the specific one."

So a wizard, is he? My assumption he is a warrior of some kind is a natural one, but I'm happy enough to have a magic user in our midst, no insult meant to the druid troll. Though I prefer to trust my sword above all else —when I'm in possession of one, that is—having some magic to throw around when times are tough or if we are faced with the same in turn is a good thing.

"How lovely," Blossom says, speaking what I'm thinking though with much more sarcasm than is in my train of thought. "Isn't it wonderful to have someone with magical experience in our company? Except when the wizard apparently doesn't know how to go about opening a simple door."

I grab her and pull her out of harm's way as the dwarf snarls at her like he'd be happy to gut her and leave her behind with the dead guard.

"Be assured, annoying halfling," he says, "that Graldor Hammercast, wizard keeper of the Basalt Hill Clan, will not be bested by a mere door."

"We'll see," she says, sticking her tongue out at him. She's obviously young, too young to be out on her own, and yet here she is. That sharp wit of hers might serve her in familiar situations, but I worry she's going to get herself into more trouble with those she's supposed to be working with let alone the guards I anticipate on the other side of the exit. "Go ahead then, dwarf. Impress us already."

He turns his back on her, though whether to keep from choking her or to do as he promised I'm not sure. If this was a less dangerous situation their exchange actually might be amusing. As it is, I'm anxious to be moving on, acutely aware of the precariousness of our position. If we're caught here in this hallway by guards of significant number, we're either going to be back in our cells in short order or very much dead. And I'm rather attached to my life right now, memories or no memories.

Something about the sensation of being trapped makes me queasy.

"Hurry it up, why don't you?" The paladin prods him with words and, from the way her hands twitch, she wants to do more than that.

"I'm working as fast as I can." He doesn't turn around until he makes a soft sound of success, though the door remains sealed and closed. He spins toward us, face creased in confidence. "There's a key we're missing," he says then, accusation in his tone, gaze falling on the halfling. "We'll need it to break the spell and move past the entry."

"What kind of key?" The paladin turns back toward the cell and the body of the hobgoblin, but I'm already looking down at Blossom as the dwarf Graldor is. Her innocent look of guilt tells me everything I need to know and more.

"Hand it over," I say, shaking her slightly from my grip on her arm.

She feigns shock and outrage, huffing a breath as she widens those big eyes at me. "How dare you accuse me of whatever it is you're accusing me."

I sigh, shake her gently again. "Blossom, the key. We don't have time for this and you know it. Where is it?"

More pouting. "Why would you assume I have anything like that?" Was she being purposely obtuse?

"You're a thief," Graldor says. "Should be about this big." He pinches his fingers together until they are an inch or so apart, then turns his hand and does the same thing, slightly longer. "A rune stone with a mark like this etched on it." He points at the door, the three circle motif in the middle and a tiny indentation at the center of them. "See anything like that?"

She jerks herself free of me and turns sideways, not meeting my eyes or his. "Maybe," she says. "What's it worth to you?"

I expect the dwarf to lose it on her, but when the tall elf grasps her by the ear and tugs hard, the halfling squeals while her captor leans close.

"Hand it over right now," she says, the song in her tone turning to a melodic threat, "or I'll clip your ears so short you'll look like a human."

Blossom gasps and stares up at the elf like she's offended her horribly. "You would *not*."

"Watch me." The elf keeps a firm hold with one hand and extends her free one, long fingertips brushing the halfling's chin. "The stone, Blossom. You might like the view, but I'm done with it. We need to get out of here."

"I was going to hand it over," the halfling's whining is a surprise, though when her elf companion lets her go she doesn't reach for the stolen property immediately. "I was just having some fun."

"We don't have the luxury of fun right now, little one," Vosh says, far kinder than I'm feeling right now, and surprising from a troll no matter what kind and gentle persona he's chosen to show to the world. "Please, can you give us the key so we can go?"

To my surprise, she fishes it out of her pocket and gives it to me before turning her back on all of us and refusing to speak. I hand it off to Graldor who scowls in her direction before spinning on the door and placing the stone in the center. It's as he described, a small, flat rectangle of some kind of stone with a triple circle in the center. Graldor places it and then turns it slowly, something clicking inside the door before it shakes just a little.

And doesn't open.

Everyone groans, but Graldor waves that off. "Silence, critics and complainers," he grumbles. "There is a step I must complete. Give me a moment." Then he snaps his fingers. "A password, of course."

"Are you any good at riddling passwords, Graldor?" Vosh sounds hesitant.

"Of course," the wizard says, blowing a bit of air between his lips like such a suggestion is a personal insult to his intelligence. "And besides, it's something fit for a stupid hobgoblin to remember. How hard can it be?" He touches the stone and speaks. "Three circles."

The door sighs and releases, faintest flare of power around the edges glowing and then it swings outward half an inch. Graldor turns to grin at all of us with smug cockiness, wrinkles forming around his dark eyes when his round cheeks lift at his glee.

"There, you see?" He hooks both thumbs into the waist band of his pants. "You're welcome."

"Allow me." The paladin pushes past all of us and I'm right on her heels, irritated she's shoved her way into the lead. This time there's no mistaking the fact I crave that position for myself. For some reason I feel like that's my place, and when I reach out to grab her hand, to slow her down, the others right behind us, I feel my grasp slow and become impossibly trapped, my fingers touching her skin and freezing there while the air around me thickens into an invisible goo and I'm caught, held rigid. At least I can breathe, but that's the extent of my movement.

"It would seem," Blossom says in her cheery voice, "it's not just hobgoblins that are stupid."

Graldor howls a low protest. "I overlooked something, that's all," he says.

"Maybe the fact we're not hobgoblins ourselves?" I'm able to turn my head, I discover, look back when Blossom's face squishes, tendons in her neck flexing, telling me she's also trapped from the head down. It could be worse for her, of course, had the spell hit at a certain general height. But it appears to affect all of us from the neck down.

Just as well. I'd rather not watch her smother while there's nothing I can do to help her or the dwarf wizard who's just four inches taller than her.

"There has to be a way out of this," the elf says. "Graldor?"

"I'm thinking," he snaps.

"Think faster." She tilts her head to one side, face leaning out as she tenses. "I hear footsteps."

Blossom opens her mouth, the obvious, "Of course you do," more than likely her choice of taunt. I shake my head at her to keep her quiet, not that silence will help. Because, a moment later, still no closer to freeing ourselves from the sticky goo of the air around us, we can only stare at the four hobgoblins who turn the abrupt corner and almost run right into us.

CHAPTER SIX

OUR ONLY SAVING GRACE becomes the previously spoken and soon to be proven stupidity of hobgoblins. Because, as they spot us, they howl their fury at our escape and, without considering our position, leap at us with the intent to attack.

I stand frozen, head turning to one side, as the descending short sword plunges in slow motion toward my shoulder, stopping inches from slicing off my left arm. So close to me that when I turn my head I could kiss the rusting blade if I so chose.

The hobgoblin who attacked me grunts when it realizes its mistake, three companions all caught in the same position in varying degrees of rigid stillness.

"I guess once the trap is sprung, it's sprung." Vosh sounds far too calm about this whole thing for my liking.

"Apparently," Graldor says, just as clinically observant, enough I want to shout at both of them to shut up as my own tension won't allow such frivolity at the moment.

"I'll crush your bones and eat the marrow and make you drink the blood of your still-pumping heart!" The hobgoblin whose sword I face seems to think it can do something about its threat while the firm hold of fear gives way and I suddenly understand Vosh and Graldor's reactions. Whether it's the creature's lisping and slightly high-pitched voice or the fact that without a way to fight, with the threat looming but as trapped as we are, I have no other outlet, humor wins. A giddy sense of comedy almost chokes me.

"You do that," I say. Blossom snorts. "Any time now."

Even the paladin grins at that, though the hobgoblin just ahead of me doesn't seem to think this is funny.

"Now what?" The paladin glares at the frothing hobgoblin whose head thrashes back and forth while it tries to free itself from the spell keeping all of us contained. The remaining two, a little further away, look stunned and scared.

"There's only one way out of this," Graldor says. "They have to release the spell."

"Never." The furious one stops fighting long enough to pant that word.

"Sir," the one in front of me says. "We can't just stay here."

"Or we could," I say. "Just wondering how long you're expecting to wait for replacements to come along and rescue you?"

From the sullen expression on the leader's face they're on their own for quite some time. Which is both reassuring and disconcerting, though once we're past them that means we have some breathing room.

"We have superior weapons," my attacker says, turning awkwardly to spit its words at its commander. "Release the spell and we'll cut them down and no one will be the wiser."

"But releasing the spell isn't instantaneous," the leader says.

"Thanks for that." I grin while Blossom giggles. Stupid hobgoblins indeed.

My attacker snarls in my face. "You just wait, you," it growls. "I'll be snacking on your liver before too long."

"Just go on the count of three," one of the others calls out. "Right, sir?"

"Three, you got it," the leader says. "That's after four?"

My jaw aches from the absurdity and the need to laugh. "I believe three comes after six," I said.

"No, it's after four," the fourth guard says.

"Isn't three first?" Blossom is oh, so helpful.

The hobgoblins mutter in their language a moment before the leader barks something and they all fall silent. In the moment it makes its decision, I see its eyes close, its lips move and know the end of the spell is coming. We all do, apparently, except for its three fellow guards who are fortunately a little slower to figure out what it's doing. That doesn't mean I'm in the clear when the sword threatening my throat starts to quiver and the shocked hobgoblin who attacked me realizes it's almost free. I'm highly motivated to move, twisting sideways when the blade begins to fall, the edge skimming past the curve of my arm and missing by the width of a breath as I push off with the balls of my feet and force myself through the last of the heavy air and impact my opponent.

This hobgoblin isn't weighed down by buckets and nor is it as surprised as the last one I brought down when I tackle it, weapon already out and in full swing. But I'm heavier than it is, the guard's shorter stature if stockier body giving way under the force of my collision, my body suddenly freed from the spell hurtling faster and harder than I might have managed otherwise.

We crash to the floor, the sounds of shouting all around me, my embed flashing red as I stab with the bone knife I still hold. The hobgoblin twists out of the way, the blade pinning one of its ears to the ground for an instant, making it howl. But it's already twining its short, powerful legs around mine and with a heave flips me over onto my back, blood spurting from its torn flesh, leaving my bone knife behind.

Roles reversed, I'm suddenly fighting it off, the sword too long to make a blow count. Its free hand catches me, the hook on its wrist slicing into my shoulder. It's my turn to use my legs, nailing it solidly between the thighs, its groan and sudden rigidity enough proof I hit where it counts. My hand finds its belt, the dagger carried there. I bury the blade up to the hilt in its side, twisting the metal as far as I can. It grates over the hobgoblin's ribs, blood gushing out over my stomach in a heated wash, the point digging around in the creature's vital organs enough that its agony of my low blow disappears. Its eyes roll back into its head and it collapses, dead weight and still oozing life blood, on top of me.

Panting, I shift it off, kicking free and leaping to my feet in time to bend and retrieve the fallen sword and swing it in the same motion, removing the head from the leader hobgoblin as it jerks Blossom forward in a two-handed grip, its gaping fangs going for her face. Its body topples to one side, away from me, the halfling jerking free of its grasping hands and ducking toward me while I spin and prepare to kill again.

I'm too late for that, though, two my final number. Vosh examines the face of one of the hobgoblins carefully before bashing its already bleeding and misshapen skull into the ground one last time. He lets it go, rubbing his hands on the rock wall as if to remove any evidence he's been in contact with the filthy thing. And the paladin rises, her hands covered in blood, the last hobgoblin dead at her feet. From the look of things she's torn out its throat with her fingers.

"Might I suggest we refrain from our desire to congratulate each other," Vosh says, "gather what we can from these four and retire to a defensible position where we can exchange more thorough information?"

"Done," I say, kicking the dead hobgoblin at my feet. Blossom is already moving, darting here and there, tucking her little hands in pockets and under tunics while the rest of us step aside and let her do her job. While picking over a dead body might be something I should do, I can't bring myself to muster the energy to do it. And though the armor they wear is of similar style to the shirt I took from our guard, I don't see the paladin helping herself, though she does claim the leader's sword while I'm happy enough with the one I've used to kill its last owner.

I glance at my arm, happy to see everything seems well, including my HW number. It's risen back to twenty-four, though why I don't know. I'm not complaining.

Graldor's possession of the rune stone is the final bone of contention. As I turn and gesture for the paladin to precede me—she's going to anyway so I might as well let her think I'm all right with it and salvage some pride at the same time—I hear Blossom complaining in the background.

"But, it's mine," she says while I move on, turning the stone corridor corner and checking out the long tunnel that stretches forward with more torches leading the way.

"You have no use for it," Graldor grunts.

"But—"

"Enough." The paladin's barked command seems to be sufficient to silence Blossom, though when I glance back I see the dissatisfied pout on her face and the smirk Graldor gives her when he pockets the rune stone in a clear show of superiority. "Move on or stay here, I couldn't care which," the paladin speaks again, tone harsh, biting, full of anger. "But I'm leaving and your petty squabbles aren't going to hold me back from finishing my task." She's as good as her word, marching off without another sign or warning.

"Which is?" I stride beside her, the first few paces half a run to catch up, sword ready, eyebrow arched in question.

"Something we can talk about when we have a safe place to do so." She increases speed and takes the lead for real and I hang back, shaking

my head, wondering why the EM on my arm
shivers and goes red.

CHAPTER SEVEN

THE CORRIDOR ISN'T AS long as I'm expecting, ending in a two way branch, one running to the right and the other slightly off to the left. I go one way and the paladin the other, without talking it out first. That at least gives me confidence she knows what she's doing aside from charging off in the lead out of some sense of urgency or whatever else drives her.

When I'm stopped by a closed door, I grit my teeth and open it, though it's already partly cracked and I can see inside enough to know I'm not walking in to my doom. Instead, I enter a small chamber with higher ceilings than I've seen previously and a row of bunks, a fire pit and a few odds and ends rounding out the contents. And, to my relief, a doorway on the far wall, firmly closed, heavy wood braced with pitted metal. Hopefully one that leads out of here, wherever here actually is.

I turn back to alert the others only to find them on my heels. They followed me, the paladin on their tail, waving at me to keep moving. When I step aside to let them pass, she shrugs.

"The other way is blocked off by a rockslide," she says.

"Something we should worry about?" I hadn't considered stone collapsing on us to be a threat, but when I let myself think about it I shudder and immediately shut down my worry. It's not like I can do anything about it if the ceiling decides to fall on me.

I enter with the paladin, Blossom squealing as she races to and then bounces on one of the bunks. She raises enough dust with her enthusiasm I worry she might catch something from the wafting scent of stirred up hobgoblin she's created. Vosh and Graldor bypass the sleeping area to the corner, the dwarf going through the remains of what has to be the hobgoblin's things until Blossom takes note he's stealing her job and joins him. Vosh seems acutely aware of his size and sits at the fire pit with his hands in his lap, staying out of the way while the elf checks the door on the other side of the room before closing it again and nodding to us.

"A corridor," she says. "Empty. For now."

While I'd like to just leave now, the fire is a welcome sight as is the pot of some kind of stew bubbling over the coals. The temptation isn't just mine. Without saying a word to each other, the elf, paladin and myself quickly barricade the doorway with one of the bunk frames. Adrenaline fading, weariness sets in and I'm happy to sink down the wall and sit on the floor with a bundle of mattress under me, the vaguely spoiled tasting stew I'm handed going down easier than it might under other circumstances.

"Just don't ask what's in it," Blossom says as she skips away to give Vosh a bowl that's ridiculously tiny in his grasp. I don't say a word, not wanting to know what I'm eating, tipping back my portion and slurping a healthy taste, swallowing despite the increasingly unappetizing odor. Food is food and my embed agrees, especially when the helpful little halfling passes around a flask of some kind of liquor. It's harsh as it burns its way down but I'm warm suddenly and much more relaxed. I groan softly while I extend my legs, crossing them at the ankles, and pass the flask along to the paladin who's chosen to perch next to me.

She salutes me as she swigs, winces, hands it on to Vosh. He does the same, a few drips squeezed past his lips, deep voice vibrating when he speaks.

"May the good grace of Eldora WorldMother lift your spirits and warm your soul." He drinks again, the elf bending her head to him.

"And on your house and hearth," she says, sipping from the flask he hands her.

"You two," Graldor says, though with good nature despite his grumbling tone, "and your earthy ways can just keep it." He chugs a swift swallow before passing it to Blossom again. Their griping seems to have ended with food, rest and drink.

"The call of WorldMother touches all hearts," the elf says, her voice taking on a particular tone, like she's prepared to teach him the error of his ways if need be.

"You're of a forest tribe?" The paladin next to me interrupts before the elf can continue her instruction.

"I am," she says, long ears sweeping back, giving her an alien appearance as much as anything else about her. Elves always make me uncomfortable with their elongated bones and frail appearing bodies. But there's nothing fragile about her, I know that from experience.

How? I wish I can remember. The elf goes on while I ponder my memory loss now that I have time to do so.

"Fleur Eldoak," she says. "Born of Wishrung Wood, ranger."

Ah, a ranger. And not an unusual choice for an elf.

"We've been introduced to our wizard," the paladin says, "and you, troll druid." Vosh nods. "And, of course, the rogue of the hour."

"At your service," Blossom peeps, winking at Graldor for using his turn of phrase.

"I'm Damaris West," the paladin says, "in the service of the crown princess."

And here I am a mere fighter thinking I should be leading. I almost snort, except they're all looking at me and I realize they're waiting for my introduction, one I hardly know how to deliver.

"I'm a bit lacking in the details," I admit. Blossom snorts, but I go on anyway. "I think my name is Webb."

"Think?" Damaris's eyes narrow, her lips pausing over the rim of the flask that's come back around the other direction to her again. "What does that mean?"

"Do any of you know how you got here?" I wait for replies as they shrug.

"The usual way," Vosh says, big hands resting between his folded legs, knuckles pressed into the rock. His skin tone is a good match, the same dull gray so his hands blend into the stone. "I was trying to break into the citadel and was captured and sent to the cell block through a magic portal."

"The same for me," Graldor says. "Caught by a spell I wasn't expecting." That fact makes him distinctly unhappy.

They all seem to agree they arrived the same way as I did. I almost ask about the delivery. The white light, the voice and the bell. Not to mention my embed. But Fleur tilts her head and observes me with her bright green eyes, unnerving me into silence.

"You have memory loss?" She sounds like she's singing the question.

"Yes," I say. "I don't know how I arrived here." Not exactly true, but I hurry on anyway. "This all feels familiar, but... I think I'm a fighter?"

Blossom taps the toe of my boot with one fingertip, points at the sword at my hip, as if I need the reminder I've killed three hobgoblins in very short order. "Safe bet, Webb."

"As for the rest..." I spread my hands in my lap. "Where are we? You mentioned a citadel?" I focus on the troll druid when he nods.

"The stronghold of the Demon King," he says.

That rings no bells whatsoever. They must see my continuing confusion because they appear at a loss to go on until the dwarf takes the plunge.

"You must be under some kind of spell," Graldor says, frowning. "I can have a look if you like?"

I shake my head, mention of the Demon King catching my attention. "Tell me more."

Vosh takes up the story after a brief look about as if the others might like to do the deed. "It's a simple tale," he says. "Not so long ago, the Cavelorn Queen, Vanarion, was struck down and lay dying at her home in Cascavel."

"No longer." Damaris twitches beside me, hands me the flask. "She's been brought here in the hope of her salvation."

I don't ask what she means by that because Vosh nods and carries on. "A minion of the

Demon King was captured, and in interrogation admitted to the act of war."

"He screamed the truth," Damaris growls.

"You were there?" I turn to her, not surprised to see the grim fury on her face.

"I conducted the interrogation," she says before falling silent and taking the flask back.

We all stare at her a long moment until she goes on, wiping her mouth with the back of her hand. "When the demon admitted his king ordered the queen's attack, the crown princess assembled the Cavelornian army and began their march here, to the citadel. But she sent me ahead to seek the Demon King and the means to kill him for what he'd done."

"Alone," Fleur says.

"How dubious," Vosh nods.

Damaris's face crumples a moment before she seems to shake off their doubt. "Perhaps she didn't order me explicitly," she says.

I take the flask and salute her, sipping the foul liquid. "I take it the rest of you are here for similar reasons?"

"Not for the queen specifically," Graldor says, though he tips his head to Damaris. "But the means to kill the Demon King? Yes, that."

"Surely your memory isn't so far lost you don't know the Soulblade?" Fleur hugs herself, staring into the fire pit and the slowly dying coals there.

Soulblade. I nod slowly, remembering the voice. "A weapon?"

"Created by the first mage of Cavelorn," Damaris says. "And the only thing that can kill a Demon King."

"Which is why he stole it from Queen Vanarion," Blossom says, voice sad and low, "and why he struck the way he did."

"He used its magic against her," Damaris says, voice catching ever so slightly. "Snuck into the palace in the dark of night, the merest scratch enough to enslave her to the blade's power. And then he left her to die, slowly from a wound no magic but the Soulblade itself can heal. Without it to reverse its attack, the queen will die."

"If the Soulblade was made by one of her own people," I say, "how can it be turned against her?"

"No one fully understands the heart of the blade," Graldor says, sounding sad about that. "The creation of it, the power it took to embed the essence of its maker into the core of it, is lost to us. All that is known is it sat in safety in the halls of Cascavel until a year ago when the new Demon King rose and, somehow, stole it from the queen." He shifts in place. "I came thinking to sneak in from beneath the city," Graldor goes on. "An old friend of mine helped build the main structure and swore to me there was a way in." He grunts, shrugs. "He lied, I suppose. Or the building's structure has been altered since."

"Dwarves," Blossom grins. "They make great friends, don't they?"

He swats at her but doesn't argue.

"I'm here for the gold," she says, as perky as ever. "And the Soulblade if I can manage it. But gold will do."

"Bratty halfling," Fleur says. "Does the safety of the queen and our world mean nothing to you?" She meets my eyes. "Graldor only told you part of what's important." If he takes offense to her statement he doesn't show it. "If the Soulblade's power is allowed to run its course and the queen dies..."

"The Demon King can use her spirit, then trapped in the heart of the sword, to unlock the power of the Soulblade for his own use." Damaris's growling tone makes her sound ferocious.

"He can call on the power of Cavelorn," Fleur says, "and command the armies of all nations, as well as those of his own kind."

"If the Demon King can find a way to command the soul of the first mage there will be nothing we can do," Damaris says. "He will open the way for his demon kin to our world and the Soulblade will be forever corrupted and our people enslaved."

"Not what Mage Borengald intended when he embedded his own soul in its length," Vosh says with sad agreement. "It was he who slew the first Demon King, dying in the process. Creating a barrier between the demons and our world with his own soul and the blade of his people."

"It's stood as a shield against their coming for a thousand years," Damaris goes on. "Only recently has the new Demon King found a way through to our world, at great cost, they say, to his own kind. But he did it, though he's only partway here. He and his people must exist in the stolen bodies of those who willingly give up themselves to host him and his minions." I can't imagine agreeing to something like that personally. "They have waited for ten centuries for the chance to return to power."

Fleur's sorrow sounds like a song. "The Soulblade's magic and the power of Borengald can free him the rest of the way if he breaks that soul's control over the sword."

"I take it he has the means to make that happen?" I shiver before clamping down on my growing anxiety.

"Harming the queen is step one," Damaris says. "Her stolen spirit might be the way to do what no one else has succeeded in doing, not even the first Demon King." I turn to speak to her, want to ask her why the Demon King didn't just kill her. Wouldn't that make more sense, rather than allowing time to do the job? There's so much more I don't know. But my tongue cleaves to my palate when I look down and notice letters and numbers etched in her forearm. Shocked, I stare at them while she tosses the now empty flask to her feet and stands, brushing her hands off on her thighs, face tight and angry. "This has been delightful," she says, voice dropping and going harsh, her strong features more like stone than flesh. "But I'm moving on now. With or without you."

CHAPTER EIGHT

I'M MUCH HAPPIER WITH a sword on my hip, even a short one fit for a hobgoblin, as we exit through the next door and into the tunnel beyond. No sleep, that would be pushing our luck, but at least food in our bellies and a hit of spirits to warm the blood has given me renewed energy.

Now that we're all at least reasonably armed, even Graldor hefting a small axe as though his dwarfish descent is more powerful than his wizard training, I feel some optimism we might actually make our way out of this prison, though I don't know that I'm as motivated to hunt down the Soulblade as the others. And yet, there's a pull forward I can't deny, an excitement that burns in my heart when I pace next to Damaris with my eyes scanning the way ahead, empty save for more torches and the roughhewn outline of the tunnel walls. I'm meant to keep going, driven by it. Amorphous and unexplained, but present. And while I can't remember why I'm here, surely their quest is my own? The voice that sent me through the light and into the cell talked of the Soulblade.

That must mean I'm heading in the right direction. I just wish I knew why. Emotional motivation might give me a boost when I need it most. I'll just have to trust that if the time comes I'm lucky enough to confront the Demon King— or unlucky as the case may be—I'll know what to do when I need to do it.

I can do little about my predicament, and so I instead allow myself to accept and move on. I observe my surroundings with a feeling of detached curiosity, senses tuned further ahead and whatever threats might be pending. Whoever built the passage to the cells wanted to ensure prisoners held there have little option when it comes to escape. The tunnel curves vaguely upward, my thighs burning slightly from the increased elevation, Graldor puffing unhappily behind me while Blossom skips forward to hold my free hand.

Startled, I look down at her, see her wink and bat her lashes before she laughs and falls back again. I can't help but smile, though I wonder at her crush and if she knows I already feel protective of her as I might a little sister.

"How goes it, Graldor?" I glance over my shoulder where Vosh takes the rear, his head just brushing the ceiling. At least it's a little higher here so he's not hunching as he had been forced to do, though I wonder if his massive stature might, at some point, become a hindrance and not a help. Though it's good to have such a big friend around when I need him, if we are forced into any kind of tight places he may become a liability.

The BL marking on my arm burns briefly and I shake off that train of thought, the faint red of the FH turning the last letter faintly to an S before shifting back again. My mind quivers with a hint of information. From faithful hero to selfish in a flash of decision. I don't know what that means really, I know so little, but it troubles me nonetheless.

Graldor responds, the small rune stone in his hand. "I think I've tapped into the magic that allows it to trap those in its vicinity," he says, a certain level of excitement in his voice that's unfamiliar from him. But discussing magic seems to stir the passion in him and he goes on with a smile on his face. "I should be able to keep us out of it, now that I've keyed the spell to ignore our particular touch."

"Should bes make me nervous." Blossom tosses her head, topknot bouncing. "Just make sure you've got all of us covered. I'm not interested in slowing down at a time when I need speed on my side." Not like her to grumble, though I remember then she likely still carries animosity for the wizard's refusal to give her the stone.

"Maybe I should set it to trap you, halfling," Graldor says in a sweet tone that makes me grin. "And leave you here for the change of guard."

She snarls something in a language I don't recognize, though the meaning is as plain in any dialect and since he's used the same tactic on her I know it's a calculated choice. I have a feeling our little halfling is much more intelligent than any of us give her credit for, including me.

"Temper, temper," Fleur says in her sing-song voice.

"Shut up," Blossom snaps.

"If you're done entertaining yourselves," Damaris snarls at them in a low tone that vibrates with annoyance, "maybe you'd all like to be quiet so we don't walk into something we're unprepared for."

"Indeed," Vosh says, though when I turn to meet his blue eyes he's grinning, the padding of his big feet a little louder than needful. He's the only one of us without a weapon, nothing of use to him in the guard room. But he's hardly without protections of his own and those massive fists and big feet are formidable enough I don't doubt he'll be fine if it comes time to fight again.

When it comes time.

Despite the paladin's harsh criticism, we encounter nothing and no one, instead coming to a halt not long later at the foot of a set of spiral stairs. It's dark, no light reaching us, and I consider going back to liberate a torch when Blossom patters past me on her furry feet and scampers upward.

"Damn her." Damaris goes after her, hand on her sword to keep it from jingling in her scabbard and I do the same, Graldor openly complaining now in dwarfish and the troll sighing at the tight space.

Fleur practically floats upward, slipping past me when I pause to scoot aside for Graldor and wait for Vosh to maneuver his big bulk around the continuing curve.

"I'll be fine," he says, only the faintest trace of frustration in his eyes, though I could be reading him wrong. He's a troll, after all.

"I'm not leaving you," I say. And when he grins I know I'm reading him just fine, thank you.

It's not a long climb, but enough that Vosh is squeezed tight by the staircase's embrace by the time we reach the group. They've stopped, whispering among themselves, while I tap Fleur on the shoulder.

"What's wrong?" I peek around her, spot the door and the sight of Blossom and Damaris arguing in heated whispers. Graldor leans against the wall with a disgusted look on his face, turning to gesture to me.

"It appears they're having a terribly timed discussion about the halfling's impetuousness," Fleur says.

I slip past her as best I can without crushing her against the stone curve and frown at the wizard who tosses his hands.

"Listen," I say to the two unhappy souls who turn to glare at me like they don't welcome the interruption, "maybe you two would like to have this conversation somewhere we're not pinned down if we're discovered. And that our troll friend isn't a target unable to protect himself."

Damaris flinches, Blossom herself looking at least momentarily contrite.

"After you," the halfling gestures at the door.

"No, please," Damaris grinds between clenched teeth. "You first. Maybe someone will kill you and save me the trouble."

The halfling rogue makes a rude gesture with her middle finger before pushing the door open and slipping around it like a shadow washed away by the sun. She moves so fast I blink, wondering for a moment if she was even there at all until she reappears, waves, disappears again.

"All clear, I'd guess," I say. "Shall we?"

"She's going to be a problem," Damaris says, eyes snapping with anger.

"Then she'll get herself killed, as you said," I shoot back. "And take care of the problem for you. But the more you try to stop her the worse it will get." That much is apparent. "Just let her do her thing and you do yours. And if she draws attention we don't want, we'll deal with it."

Damaris looks like she wants to argue, but Graldor grunts and pushes past her, out the door, Fleur following. I let the paladin go with them, waiting again for Vosh who sighs deeply, voice pitched low and quiet.

"I fear our halfling friend is less of an issue than Damaris herself." He sounds slightly guilty saying so.

I'm thinking the exact same thing, guilt free, however. But this isn't the time or place to fret over it. There's always the option to cut ties and move on myself, though I feel comfortable with this group of fellow adventurers. As if this is how I'm meant to proceed. And so, until I feel otherwise, I'll stick things out and see where their association takes me.

All the way to the Soulblade?

I pass through the door with that question on my mind, my arm aching as the tattoo glows faintly in answer.

CHAPTER NINE

WHEN I STEP AROUND the half open door and into the chamber beyond, I pause and observe where I now found myself, sense of danger low enough it feels like I can take the time to do so. Odd, this room, less hacked from stone like the rest of the places we've been and more polished, it seems, with a large and elaborate fountain in the center, water bubbling up from the pool surrounding a plain statue. In fact, it's more than plain, it's blank, faceless, sexless, without attire or any kind of distinguishing features. As though the sculptor lost interest after forming the initial shape. So unusual considering the carefully carved blocks that fit together to make the fountain's curving containment, the dark blue stone far more decorative than the utter nothing standing in its center.

Blossom perches on the edge of the pool of water, sniffing it a moment before cupping some in her hand and slurping it down. She spins and beams at us, waving us forward, while Damaris, circling past a flickering torch and moving slowly toward a closed, wooden doorway on the left, rolls her eyes at me.

"It's delicious!" The halfling lies on her belly on the stone lip and drinks deeply of the water, little feet swinging as she does. Far too innocent seeming for a thief, and much more an act I'm starting to see through than perhaps she's aware of. I can understand how she more than likely gets away with far more than she would if she were of some other race. A healthy advantage for the halfling and fair enough when size is an impediment to other callings.

Fleur joins her, one fingertip touching the bubbling water. She smiles then, nods. "It's clear," she says. "It must feed up from some deep spring far under the rock." Her long, slim hand forms a cup and she sips from it. "Refreshing."

I have to admit I'm really thirsty now, the liquor I've drunk leaving a terrible burned taste in my mouth. It was fine at the time of imbibing, but a long, deep drink of something cold and fresh would certainly hit the spot. The little bit of water I'd had in my cell feels like forever ago and though the stew has settled in my stomach and is doing its part to keep me going, the call of the water is undeniable.

I wait, though, stubborn perhaps? I'm not too big to admit it, nor that it's not until Damaris leaves her examination of the doorway without opening it and joins the others and takes a drink, her eyes locked on me, that I sample it at the same time she does.

Yes, stubborn. And other things I really need to set aside but can't seem to when it comes to the paladin. Though why I would need to prove myself to anyone, especially the special envoy of the crown princess, is beyond me.

Maybe it's more than that. The fact she has a tattoo like mine? I need to find time to ask her about it. She appears to have memories I don't. She might know what it means and why it seems to track everything I do with careful attention.

I hesitate after my first drink as the PH in my embed shivers but doesn't change or glow. I suppose simply drinking at this stage isn't going to be enough to help me level up. That phrase makes me pause. Level up to where? It means something, and it's important. It's a core principle to everything I'm doing here. But what does it mean? And why is it so vital I keep moving forward in more ways than one?

Blossom finishes first, booping Vosh on the nose with one finger as he kneels next to the fountain to drink, evading Damaris—choosing her side on purpose to circle, I'm positive of that—and past the paladin toward the other side of the fountain. At first I think she's going to examine the second closed door directly across from the first, fountain directly between them. Instead, though, she skirts the edge and heads for the far end of the room and the third and final door we've yet to explore.

And squeaks in surprise as she seems to impact something before falling backward with the most startled look on her face, landing hard on her posterior.

Graldor laughs, a guffaw of harsh humor, while Blossom's cheeks redden and she's scrambles to her feet, rubbing her bottom with one hand as if injured.

"Trip and fall over those feet at last, halfling?" He wipes water from his beard with one hand.

She shakes her head, frowning, easing forward, hands raised. I join her and am next to her when she stops, her fingers running sideways, up and down, but moving no further ahead.

I touch the place above her fingers and feel the invisible barrier she impacted, Damaris appearing on my other side, doing the same thing.

"Some kind of shielding?" She meets my gaze, her own troubled.

"Well, obviously," Blossom says, one hand on her cocked hip. "I guess you never claimed to be brilliant."

Damaris's clenched fists, I believe, are the only thing keeping her from screaming at the halfling and her attitude. "Any idea where it comes from or are you going to just be rude to everyone because you're embarrassed you fell down?"

I shouldn't laugh because it's not funny, but it's so true I can barely contain myself. Blossom splutters a moment, arms crossing sullenly over her chest while she tips her chin toward the barrier.

"Ask the wizard," she snarls, turning her back on the paladin and stomping away. Not back toward the fountain and the others, but sideways, to the door that's in line with the barrier, on this side of it at least.

I go with her if only to keep her from hurting herself again and when she notices I'm at her back when she reaches for the door handle she scowls at me before she pinks again and looks away. Has she learned a lesson from her impetuousness? Not likely, though she does open this door more slowly than I've observed her take on any task in the past and peeks around the corner of it before stepping inside.

I'm right behind her, hand on my sword. There's no need for a weapon here, however. Bunks line the walls, these places of rest nothing like the horrible huddle the hobgoblins used below. The wooden frames are piled with blankets and pillows, and a large cushion filled pit in one corner looks coincidentally troll sized. Blossom runs off to investigate with the renewed interest of an eager child, all forgiven and forgotten in her mercurial way of being.

I don't protest her innocent fun, wondering when the next time will come she can romp with such abandon. We explore a few minutes, Blossom's part played out in a bouncing, squealing playtime in the middle of the cushions while I search under a few mattresses and inside blankets. But aside from a place to sleep, the place is empty.

"Guard's quarters?" That doesn't feel right to me. There's no stench of hobgoblin here, no reek of their fetid flesh on the bedclothes. And there's the exact number we require, including the pit for our troll friend. Odd and makes me uncomfortable, though when Graldor joins us he seems pleased by the setup.

Even Damaris isn't suspicious enough for my liking, Fleur and Vosh taking their turn to look around. I leave them, the paladin trailing after me, and cross in front of the fountain, glancing up at it as we pass. Wait, wasn't it blank the last time I looked? How strange, there seems to be the vague form of a nose, fingers on the hands, even the faint outline of clothing. I must have missed those details when I first entered.

I pause with my hand near the handle of the door, raise an eyebrow to Damaris who waves off my silent question with a twist to her lips.

"Just open it," she says.

I do, carefully, not as eager as Blossom to lurch from one place to another as she always appears to be. And gape in shock at the sight of a banquet table overflowing with food, the smell assaulting my senses so abruptly I find I'm drooling while the paladin next to me does the same.

CHAPTER TEN

"THIS MUST BE A dream." Damaris sounds enthralled briefly before shaking herself, frowning.

"Too good to be true?" I shrug. "If it's a threat, I don't understand it."

She bites her lower lip, hesitates and I know what she's thinking. We need to close and bar this door just in case. Not let the others in, let them see. At the very least, warn them not to eat the food. Then again, if Graldor senses no magic outside the invisible shielding keeping us from moving forward, what's the harm?

"Too many unanswered questions," I say. "We should talk about this."

"Agreed," Damaris says, mouth still open to go on, a breath drawn. Even as something small and stealthy slips between us with a piercing squeal of delight.

I shouldn't be surprised Blossom streaks toward the table, feet padding on the woven carpet, throwing herself into a chair she instantly stands on, handfuls of food grasped and thrust into her mouth as she quickly mows through a selection of what smells like the most succulent and delicious dishes I've ever had the pleasure of considering for dinner.

Long before Damaris and I can do a thing to stop her.

No time to say a word or warn her, and frankly I don't want to anymore. Seeing her eat all that deliciousness sends jealous ripples through me. And yet I have just enough self-restraint left to hang on long enough for Blossom's impetuousness to show good or ill. I'm hoping, my stomach rumbling in need the rotten stew below didn't fill, that she's not about to fall over and die on us.

Blossom sees us staring and, for a heart stopping moment, she freezes. Her hands clutch into little claws, eyes widening as she struggles for breath and I know the worst has happened while she tumbles sideways into the chair and gasps her last.

Only to sit up again with a wink and goes back to eating all over again while Damaris swears next to me. We're firmly set aside when Vosh lumbers his way past and takes a seat at the end of the table, literally taking up the entire end with his bulk, reaching forward with his two massive arms and sweeping the majority of the food toward him.

"Hey!" Blossom tries to nab a plate of what looks like rare red meat slathered in gravy from his grasp but he's faster than he looks and she backs off, still chewing what's in her mouth.

Graldor and Fleur join us, the dwarf rubbing his hands together and hurrying to the table, but the elf hesitates and I find I'm with her, though my mouth continually waters in a way I'm sure will drown me if I don't swallow often enough.

"What is this place?" She shivers slightly, looks around, green eyes near glowing in the light of the dangling chandelier. It's a comfortable enough room with a large fireplace and tall ceilings, stone carved walls, candles in sconces topped by flames dancing their welcome to the table. All together a calm and happy kind of place, perfect for a satisfying meal. "Where does the food come from?"

I shake my head, bite the inside of my cheek, feel the compulsion to eat fade enough a scowl pulls my brows together. This is distinctly odd to find at the head of a prison block. Isn't it?

"Excellent question," Damaris says, though she's swaying toward the table. "Any guesses?"

"Magic," the elf shrugs. "What else?"

"I believe the more important question is why." I lock my knees to keep from giving in to the return of my stomach's siren call. It's so hard to watch Graldor slather what has to be fresh butter all over a giant, steaming tuber bursting from the skin and eat it with one giant bite. I can almost taste it on my own tongue and have to turn sideways and fix my gaze on Fleur to remain in one place.

"Could this be for the guards?" I doubt that question even as I speak it, wishful thinking from a starving man. And I am starving suddenly, as if I've never eaten before in my life. Just a snack, that's all I need. A few bites here and there. Nothing excessive. And there's so much available, though the others are eating it, all of it and if I don't hurry I won't get anything. I hear the sound of slurping and resist turning around, knowing the sight of Vosh inhaling everything in sight will break my resolve.

There has to be something wrong with this feeling I'm fighting.

"Then why did they have their own meal cooking below?" Damaris seems hesitant, swaying herself, swallows and shrugs. "The others are eating and show no ill for it." She's making an excuse, one I want to agree with. What's the harm? "And we can use the strength good food will give us, I'm sure. None of us has had a decent meal in days." She sounds perfectly happy talking herself into dinner.

Damaris seems to have made up her mind, smiling when she leaves us. I watch her go, longing in my heart, but Fleur continues to watch and pause and I can't bring myself to abandon her just yet.

"Is there something here, Fleur?" Can she sense it?

When she meets my gaze, I see her own hunger there and that makes me even more nervous, enough to cut the desire I have to fill myself to the brim on the bounty on the table.

"I fear we're missing something," she says and leaves me to go to the banquet despite her words.

Groaning, feet betraying me, I join her and help myself to a slab of fresh bread that Blossom fights me for, a pat of butter I manage to nab before Graldor liberates the entire crock, a slab of some kind of red meat and a scoop of fluffy potatoes that fit nicely together. And then I force myself to step back, back again, one more time, and out the door, into the fountain room. I perch on the edge and eat my meal, longing for more even after my stomach groans its fullness and holding myself in place until the urge passes.

It releases me suddenly, in a rush of exhale, almost as if someone decided I wasn't worth holding onto anymore. That alone raises my level of worry to insistent prodding. I need to get up, go talk to Damaris, the others. That food, that room, all of this. We're meant to stay here, on this side of the invisible barrier. And the lure of dinner, of offered rest, surely that's something meant to trap us, isn't it?

Before I can act on my train of thought, I waver, suddenly weighted down by the need to sleep, as I would after a big and satisfying meal. Only this grows more powerful, as the thirst had, I realize, as my hunger did, until I'm struggling with it. A deep lethargy falls over me, a need to lie down so powerful I sigh heavily and run one hand over my tired eyes to rub them open again. So strange this sensation of sudden weariness, washing away everything, including my need to get up and talk to the paladin and the elf. About what again? There was something bothering me, I just can't recall clearly what. Well, my memory is an issue, so likely it's nothing important after all.

Maybe I'll get up and find a bunk and have a lovely, long nap. I've earned it, I think.

Before I go, I turn and take a handful of fresh water, about to drink, splash some on my skin to jar me awake enough to make the walk across the room to the far door when my gaze falls on the feet of the statue and I freeze into shocked awareness.

Boots. It's wearing boots. And not just any footwear, no. However it's possible, the ones on its feet look just like mine.

CHAPTER ELEVEN

A S I LOOK UP I realize it's not just the boots, but my pants, my sword at my side, everything about me mimicked in the newly shaped statue that used to bear nothing but vague human form. And, as I stare in utter shock at the transformed stone, it shifts from what must be my normal, level expression, longish hair hanging over my forehead, to another more familiar face. Within moments it's Damaris looking out over the room, carved in stone, and then, as I begin to grasp what I'm seeing, the tall form of the paladin turns to the slim and delicate Fleur.

Faster and faster the stone statue shifts from one to another, would be hilarious to me if it weren't so creepy, when Blossom's small form lurches upward into the hulking body of Vosh. Weariness washes over me in a fresh wave of dizzying assault while my visage appears yet again on the rock before it turns once more to Damaris and onward through our party.

I step up onto the edge of the fountain, feel myself sway with the need to lie down and realize this thing, this stone creation, has to be tied to what's happening to me, if not completely to blame. But when I press both hands to its morphing rock, oddly warm and pliable and making my skin creep from the contact, and try to push it off its base, my arm tingles. I look down at my embed to see the PH vibrating, glowing red.

And it strikes me. I'm not strong enough to tip it over, to do what I need to do to shake myself loose—all of us, I now suspect as Damaris's grim face looks back at me in stone. But I know someone who is.

My only worry is he's too far gone into this weariness dragging at my limbs and my mind I won't be able to stir him into action before we're all lost to what will likely be an endless sleep.

Still fighting the lethargy with a focus that gives me the power I need to move, I return to the buffet room. To find Graldor, to ask him first before recruiting my troll friend, if the magic I'm now sure influences me can be countered. Only to spot him in his chair, head back, snoring with tremendous volume, his beard heavy in his lap. The others seem about as weary as I feared would be the case, heads drooping and I have to fight my own need to sit, to join them and rest my head if only for a moment. Instead, I pinch myself hard on the inside of my elbow and, the jolt of pain momentarily perking my energy, I stride to the wizard and grasp his shoulder, shaking him hard enough to wake him under normal circumstances.

But it's apparent as Blossom's head thuds to the polished wood, a tiny smile on her little lips, this is no ordinary sleep. They are firmly in the grasp of whatever crushes my own will to remain awake. Graldor manages a grumbling mumble under his breath before turning sideways in his chair, tilting himself away from me, and snuggling down with his hands folded under is cheek, resting on the arm of the large seat.

"You have to wake up," I say, "all of you." My words sound slurred, my energy flagging again. I purposely ram my fisted knuckles into the side of Graldor's chair, the pain sending shooting sparks up my forearm and making me yip but shaking off the call of sleep threatening me.

"In a bit," Vosh says, big head dipping while he waves me off like lifting his arm is far too much effort to expend. But he is awake, thankfully, not lost like the wizard. And that means my vague and fading plan my sleepy brain is losing to weariness still has a chance. If I can get him moving before it's too late.

"No, now." I inhale and exhale heavily, forcing more breath into my lungs, trying to spike my adrenaline. Wait, what's adrenaline? I don't have time to ask that question of myself, or why I understand more oxygen to my bloodstream will help keep me awake.

Fleur is the only one who seems at my level of awareness, her thin face pinched when she blinks rapidly and shakes her head as if to stave off sleep. "Something's wrong," she says.

I refrain from a sarcastic comment only because speaking has become wearisome and I need to guard my strength. "The statue," I gasp, barely able to get those two words out.

"What about it?" Damaris's face wavers between interest and giant yawns that she covers with a fist. "We can deal with it when we get some rest."

"Since when," I force out, "is a paladin of the Cavelorn willing to let every single person in her party sleep and not one of us assigned watch? In an enemy fortress in unknown circumstances?"

That challenge seems to reach her. Damaris repeats my own effort, pinching herself sharply and sitting up. Blossom snores in soft counterpoint to Graldor, one on either side of the table while the paladin nods to me. "What about the statue?"

I'm losing my train of thought. "Magic," I say. "Sleep magic. Need to stop it somehow." I can't put together much more, instead turn to find Vosh slowly toppling to one side. And, as he does, my plan returns to me in a rush. I have a renewed thought, knowing I should have gone to him in the first place, struggling with the exhaustion and my mental control. I hurry to him this time before I can stumble and fall or forget again what I had in mind. "Get up," I say.

"Leave me be, Webb," he mumbles, blue eyes closing.

"Vosh, I need you to get up." I prod him with one foot, heart palpitating against my continuing upright position. We're almost out of time.

"Sleepy," he whispers. "Later."

Instinct strikes, though my heart aches for what I'm about to do. "Lazy, dirty, filthy creature. You're not one of us. Get up and get out!" I finish that statement with a firm kick to his shoulder. Painful enough for my poor, abused toes, though I doubt it harms him physically. It's not meant to. I don't want to hurt him. I just want him angry enough to get up.

Damaris stares at me, Fleur too, like I've lost my mind and I likely have. But I need to trust my gut and it's telling me what to do as clearly as I can interpret it. That a furious troll on the edge of sleep might lose the refinement he's gained. Could, perhaps, fight off a spell like this one if his baser instincts are woken. Maybe. If we're lucky and he doesn't snap and kill me before I can lure him to the statue.

Vosh's big eyes open and he fixes me with a glassy stare. "What? What did you say?" My effort fell well short of what I'd hoped. I need to up my game.

"You heard me, you disgusting filth bag of rotting uselessness," I snap, the challenge giving me the bit of a boost I've been needing. My blood zings a moment as I draw my sword and poke him with it. Not that the blade will do much more than my booted toes. His skin is tougher than it looks, not stone but close enough. "I've had enough of your stench following us around. Pathetic monster, you revolt me." I wince at my words. I sound like a bad sonnet some bard with terrible talent has penned. Still, it's all I have in me at the moment so it'll have to do.

Vosh's blue eyes blink, faint red glowing in their depths. Apparently my best is good enough. "I don't understand, Webb," he says, but there's anger there. Good. I need to stoke that fire. "This isn't you talking."

"It's me more than it's ever been," I say. "Now get out before the sight of you makes me puke."

It's working, it's actually working. The troll begins to rise, though the red in his gaze increases faster than I expected. The ancient rage of his people wakes within him as reason goes to sleep, and I've set off a chain reaction I hope I can direct and forgive myself for later. For now, I step away while he rises to his full height—an unseen effort until now and impressive, mightily so—before he staggers as if even his ancient warrior blood fails under the pressure of the spell controlling us.

I have no doubt now it's a spell, though I'm at a loss to figure out its powers right now beyond its drive to put us to sleep. And I have zero interest in finding out—or not finding out—

what it will mean if we fall to its call to slumber. Instead, I back away from Vosh who takes a step toward me, one giant hand fisted at his side.

"How dare you talk to me like that, puny human." His voice takes on a guttural echo most people would associate with trolls, something absent until now from his smoothly cultured tone. The stone tint of his skin darkens toward brown, all refinement vanishing while his base instincts rise to the surface. I know he'll despise himself when this is done, if we survive it. But I have no choice.

I didn't notice Damaris's approach and actually start in fright as she speaks beside me, thankful for the new shot of fear that wakes me further. "You're still here?" She throws a small piece of fruit at him, splattering against his knee and dripping red juice to the floor. She turns her head and meets my eyes, her own full of worry but trusting I know what I'm doing though maybe she shouldn't. "Kill the troll!"

I didn't expect things to go that far or to escalate to death threats so quickly, but it has the desired effect my own insults failed to create. Vosh transforms from grumpy troll to bellowing monster in about a heartbeat and any weariness still holding me is shattered as I turn, Damaris beside me, and run for the exit and the main room.

My goal is the statue, the fountain, of course. The paladin at my side skirts the table, the thundering footfalls of the troll pursuing us. She skids and slides on a bit of discarded food and I almost stop to help her when she waves me off.

"Keep going!" She rolls under the table, out of harm's way—at least, I hope so—and with the BL tattoo itching and burning I dive out the door and into the other room.

The door behind me groans, the sound of wood splintering while I leap three steps faster than I've ever moved in my life, my feet slipping a moment on the edge of the fountain, enough it sends me sprawling into the water with a mighty splash. The cold helps wake me, though as my mouth fills with the clear fluid I feel lethargy take me and smother me.

I blink underwater, the towering troll appearing over my head through the crystal liquid, red eyes blazing when he lifts both arms and brings them down in a mighty blow on either side of me, the water surging and spitting me out. I feel myself flung much like a child's doll up and over his shoulder from the force of the ejection, twisting in midair and falling on my hip and arm while I watch him spin, hands held upward in a smashing stance, his fist errantly catching the torso of the statue in the middle of the fountain.

Something booms beneath me, like the impact is a blow struck to the heart of the world. And then the statue topples in slow motion, water pouring out of the gaping hole near Vosh's knee where his first blow took out a giant chunk of rock. The statue's face morphs to blank once again just as it tumbles sideways out of the edge of the fountain and crashes to the floor.

For the briefest of moments, my head aching with the intense need to sleep, my heart slowing despite my fear and the impending looming of the troll's approach, I'm sure I see the statue's now detached head morph into a screaming woman's before it's blank again and everything shifts—

CHAPTER TWELVE

I SIT UP, RUBBING my arm and looking down at the glowing white letters and numbers as they adjust themselves. Apparently my plan to stop the statue and its magic has increased my ME by one number and I'm now a thirteen. *Mental*, my mind whispers. The use of intelligence despite my circumstances has given me a new advantage. My head aches a little though the clarity I've returned to is likely the cause.

It's a slow climb to my feet while Vosh sloshes his way out of the water still leaking from the gap in the fountain, big head down and shaking slowly from side to side, his massive hands clenched into fists at his sides. The others emerge from the feast door but I'm focused on the troll and his slumped shoulders, his lowered face, worried now as he shivers all over I still have to face his wrath.

Instead, when he raises his chin and meets my eyes, his are blue again, the raging red fire long gone. But sorrow has replaced his fury, worse to me than any deadly threat. I knew he'd be unhappy with this plan, the only viable option or not. When in the short time I've known him has the state of his soul become more valuable than the condition of my hide? Apparently the BL designation has something to do with it because it no longer reads FH but now sits at HH. From faithful hero to heartless in a single decision. My mind whispers the shift has to do with my own heart and I believe it because the guilt I feel is less than it should be.

"Well done, you two." Damaris treats the last few minutes like we planned it instead of me prodding my new friend into reverting back into his monstrous heritage. Yes, it saved us from the spell of the fountain, the statue now shattered and useless on the floor. But what damage have I done to him and the connection he has to his own power as a druid?

"What happened?" Blossom yawns, blinks, scratches at one armpit in absent confusion. "I was having the best dream."

"We were under the influence of some kind of magic," I say while Graldor stomps forward, bending to examine the fallen statue, his face crinkling under the thick hair of his beard and heavy eyebrows.

"How did I miss this?" He kicks the head, the stone tumbling away with a cracking sound while it bounces off the toe of his boot. "Devouring spell, tied to sleep. A sorceress, if I'm reading her magic rightly, trapped here by whoever set this spell. If we'd been taken fully, none of us would have woken." He pales, glancing back into the room he just left, one hand on his stomach. "That food we ate?"

"Would have eaten us in return." Fleur sounded like it was no big deal while I winced inwardly before sighing.

"We have Vosh to thank for saving us," I say, knowing my attempt to buoy his state of mind won't help. Nothing will but his own courage and strength to move past what I've done to him.

"I did nothing." He sounds like himself again, though far more subdued than before. The troll turns from me, stares down into the water and the others go on about their business as if they have no idea what just happened to him, unconcerned for his state of mind and spirit. Because they don't understand, I suppose, all but Damaris who helped me prod him into his fury. Still, it's my responsibility and I need to find a way to make it up to him if I can.

While the paladin leads the others away from the fountain, toward the banquet room and possible provisioning in the hope the offered food is no longer tainted with magic, I pass the statue and tentatively attempt to breach the barrier that knocked Blossom on her backside. But when I hesitantly approach, Vosh's deep voice interrupts my caution.

"It's gone," he says. "With the spell and the statue's control. We can move on now." He sighs deeply. "The hobgoblins knew not to touch the water, the food, sleep in the beds. When we gave in to the lure and drank, we sealed our fate."

I can't help but think he's talking about himself more than us as a group. Is there a fate he's been trying to escape I don't know of? And then it hits me. Strikes a blow like none other. He's a troll. Surely those instincts that roused him from his sleep and saved us aren't just a peripheral irritant. Does he fight against those feelings, that need to revert to his true nature, on a constant basis? And have I irreparably harmed him in forcing him to abandon the troll he's become?

I turn toward him, hand on my hilt to keep my sword from swinging and to give me somewhere to put it so I don't run it through my hair in agitation and regret. "Vosh."

He shakes his head, moves to join me in slow, deliberate steps, huge feet soft on the floor. It amazes me how agile he seems despite his massive size, how quietly he can move. When he comes to stand at my side, one hand rises and gently settles on my shoulder. Correction, two fingers. His hand could easily engulf my entire upper body if he really tried. "Webb, I understand. And I'm grateful for your quick thinking. My heritage isn't lost on me and nor am I in denial how close to the surface the monster in me lives. I just wish..."

"So do I." I hesitate a moment before rushing on. "You saved all of us. We'd be lost without you. And though I know what I did is unforgivable, I'd do it again."

Vosh's attempt at a smile is slightly horrifying, though the spark in his eyes makes me feel better about what I've done to him.

"I think someone else went against his nature to save us," he says, far more insightful than I've given him credit for. I rub at the altered BL ranking on my arm as he goes on. "For that I will remain grateful. I blame you not, my friend. And there are times when a troll's deep rage is a blessing in disguise. We will call it that in this instance and talk of it no more." I don't think he can brush it off that easily, but if he wants to try, that is up to him. "I shall meditate on my loss of control and strive to do better."

I could have argued with him, talked of his weariness, of the spell's controls, that he likely couldn't have stopped the reaction. Instead, I let him have his quiet and his time to think and hate that I feel like a coward for doing so even while knowing it's my own form of punishment for treating my friend like a tool.

My arm shivers and I look down to find my BL is back to FH. At least something positive has come from it, perhaps? Though I meant what I said and wonder what that says about me.

The others emerge once more from the banquet room, small sacks made from napkins holding provisions and, with a flourish from Blossom, a wine flask. But when Damaris scoops it out of her hands and opens the nozzle, the halfling's protests are ignored while the paladin then empties the dark red drink before rinsing the skin in the fountain and refilling it.

She smacks the thief in the chest with the still dripping skin, a grin on her face while Blossom's breath oofs out of her mouth at the impact.

"Stay sober, little one," Damaris says before whistling as she strides past. The look Blossom shoots her could have cut her open from neck to hip given the right opportunity and weapon.

I turn from my own grin, happy to be moving on, to find Graldor on his hands and knees near the chest of the fallen statue. He's digging inside it with a dagger and whispering words over the stone. When it cracks, the sound is loud enough to make all of us jump, even Vosh, whose rumbling protest makes goosebumps stand up on my arms.

Graldor holds up a small, black stone about the size of his fist. It flickers once with a pale blue light before falling still. "Any magic is helpful magic in the right hands." He stands, firmly pocketing the core of the statue while Blossom's acquisitiveness shows in her narrowed eyes and her clutching hands now grasping the edges of the water skin so tightly I can see her knuckles have turned white.

"Time to move on." Damaris leads the way and I'm content to follow this time, to let her take point while I ponder this last challenge.

That's what it feels like, a task, a puzzle to be solved and makes me wonder if there are more such ahead and, if so, what their meaning might be.

CHAPTER THIRTEEN

THEIR ARGUING STARTS UP almost immediately. We're barely in the tunnel past the third door at the other side of the room when Graldor snarls and spins on Blossom who gazes up at him with her most innocent look. Surely a sign she's up to no good.

"Hands off," the dwarf wizard snaps. "I catch you in my pockets again, little thief, and I'll seal your mouth shut."

"I have no idea what you're talking about." She sniffs as she strides past him, water skin now slung over one shoulder, but I catch her wink and grin over her shoulder, the way one hand slides into her pocket and I sigh over the pending drama.

"Hand it over." I close the distance quickly, now directly behind Damaris, Graldor pushing up against me as he attempts to reach around me to grasp the halfling. She darts sideways, tucking herself against my hip and out of his range while Fleur hangs back with Vosh and Damaris scowls at me over one shoulder.

"If you don't mind," she snaps, "we're heading into unknown territory and I could use the help."

I shrug but address Blossom again instead. "Just give it back, would you?"

She blinks her large eyes at me while the dwarf swears softly and digs into his pocket with a grimace. "I'm innocent, I tell you."

"You're a thief," the wizard grunts the obvious like it should be a surprise accusation, lunging for her while I hold him off and the paladin in the lead sighs heavily like this is my fault. I didn't recall agreeing to wrangle a pair of spoiled children when I had them all freed not so long ago. "Who can't use the magical items you stole from me. And are likely going to lose or damage said items so I can't use them either. Give them back."

She shuffles sideways, tries to shift around me, but I have a hand on the back of her shirt and Fleur quickly steps up to fill in the gap between me and Vosh who's closed the distance. Blossom sees she's cornered and instantly pouts, but she hands off the rune stone and the heart of the statue both, sticking her tongue out at first Graldor and then me as we exit the end of the tunnel suddenly.

I look up, nearly too late, Damaris hissing softly while Graldor, his head down, hands eagerly stowing his returned prizes, almost steps forward one too many times. Both of my hands instinctively fall on his shoulders, jerking him backward from the sudden, deep plunge he was about to take over the edge of the quiet, underground chasm.

"Oaks preserve us," Fleur whispers while my pounding heart echoes in my head and I look up and around at the shocking sight of the towering cavern before us. "Well caught, Webb."

Graldor shakes off my grasp but nods his head, backing slowly toward the mouth of the tunnel again. Barely a stride from the edge the ground drops off, into darkness so deep and profound I'm positive there's no end to the fall. I have zero desire to find out if I'm right.

It's dark in here, though there's enough ambient light from the walls, a faint glow almost like natural iridescence, I can begin to make out shapes in the distance. As I blink into the low illumination, I realize I'm looking at a bridge, narrow and made of stone, the head of which begins a few steps away along the edge of the cavern wall. An arching entry of stone stands over this end, climbing upward in graceful welcome. Closer inspection shows the ledge we stand on continues past the bridge entry and, when I turn to look in the opposite direction, curving away to my left, I realize it does the same that way, too.

"The bridge is blocked by something." Fleur points while Damaris squints and shakes her head and I admit I'm doing the same. I can barely see this end of it, let alone the full expanse or how far we have to go to cross. It feels like miles, though it's doubtful that's true.

"How far does it go, Fleur?" Damaris turns to the elf and asks the very question I'm pondering but the ranger shrugs.

"The full way across," she says and it's unclear if she's being purposely obtuse. "Perhaps a hundred feet? There's a tunnel at the other end. I'm assuming it's an exit."

"And the blockage you see?" I wish I had her keen sight, hating being lost in the dimness and relying on someone else for such vital information.

"Some kind of boulder or stone formation," Fleur says.

"Agreed," Vosh nods. "Though its shape is irregular. Perhaps a rock fall from above has created a barrier."

"And possibly weakened the bridge." Blossom shivers next to me, so close to me again I can feel her little body shake. "Is there another way across?"

Graldor pokes her. "Afraid, thief?"

"Cautious," she snaps back. "No rogue worth her weight takes risks if she can find a safer path to the same result."

"We could try following the narrow way around the cavern." Fleur points and I'm feeling a bit more confident knowing she can see where that path leads. I need to learn to trust. "But as far as I can tell, neither direction ends at the other side. From what I can see, there are only other doors."

"Two on the left," Vosh says, "and one on the right."

She checks again and nods to him. "Correct."

"Can we make it past the barrier on the bridge?" Damaris seems impatient despite the fact if we've learned anything it's rushing into things can only get us deeper into trouble. Surely she knows better? Even Blossom is preaching a bit of care and if she's nervous, the paladin has to listen to reason.

"I'm not sure," Fleur says. "At least, I know I could climb it. But the rest of you?" She glances back at Vosh, lowering her lashes a moment. "Apologies, friend troll."

"None necessary," he says. "There's a good chance if the bridge is damaged from a rock fall that my weight could put the rest of you in jeopardy anyway. And, if not, any barrier will likely be of little consequence compared to my strength." Practical even in the face of the possibility he may have to remain behind? He's a bigger person—no slight intended—than I am.

But I'm not so sure I'm happy to hear that hint of something uncomfortable in his voice. Why does he sound relieved by the prospect of staying here? "We're not leaving you behind," I say then, understanding it even as I speak in a rush, temper heated at the thought.

Vosh seems startled then nods to me. "Thank you," he says. "But you may not have a choice."

"There's always a choice." I turn to Damaris. "As I see it, we have a few options."

She nods, eyes tight in the corners, dark brows drawn together. At some point her tight bun has come loose and the long, thick ponytail of red hair spills over her shoulder, masking the dragon's face on her surcoat. "Split up," she says. "Two check out the right, two the left and the other two take the bridge. Meet back here and report on our findings."

My stomach flexes at the thought of doing so but I don't argue. "Or we all go right, or left, or over the bridge and explore together."

"We'll cover more ground and faster in pairs," Graldor says.

"And put ourselves at greater risk if something happens," Fleur murmurs.

"The bridge is the most obvious exit," I say, disliking all options. I scratch at the embed in my arm as the BL quivers in response to thinking about breaking up our little party and accept its warning. "Why don't we send the lightest two forward to inspect the rock fall and go from there?"

Everyone nods their agreement while my stomach unknots from its clenched state and the ME and EM on my arm quiver this time. Mental and emotional influence over the rest of the group has my implant tingling. No change in numbers but the faint white glow is encouraging. If the others notice my embed they don't comment. Does that mean they either don't see it or have their own so they don't care? Before I can bring it up, Blossom turns and heads for the bridge, the others going after her and I rub one more time at my forearm while trying not to worry too much about what the embed really means.

Time enough to ponder it when we're free.

I pause at the head of the bridge, Fleur and Blossom already partway across, light on their feet while I stare down into the darkness past the carved arching entry of the span and realize I'm not going to shed my questions so easily. What does the embed mean? Where did it come from? And why do I feel like I'm a mouse in a maze, like I'm caught in some trap I need to find my way out of? All for what? Who is behind what's happening to me and why, why can't I remember anything?

Vosh's deep gasp next to me jerks my head up, pulls me from my slowly spiraling melancholy and back into the moment as he lurches forward a step, toes brushing the edge of the bridge, one arm extended, utter shock and a hint of fear on his face as if he's only just noticed something we missed.

"Come back!" His deep voice booms at the exact moment the elf and the halfling reach the mound of fallen rocks just visible to my adjusting vision in the distance and the darkness.

Too late, they are already climbing the stones, small figures agile on the rocks. At least, they attempt to. But when they begin their ascent my aching eyes seem to play tricks on me even while the troll at my side stretches upward to his massive height and bellows out a roar that echoes back from the walls of the cavern, swallowed by the black below and above. Has he reverted again? Do we need to fear him? Has the spell somehow taken hold or has he lost control of his base instincts?

Those questions race through my mind faster than I can think them, silenced when something answers the troll's challenge, something that moves and discards the elf and halfling like toys before exploding upward to tower over the

center of the bridge and my fallen friends while
Vosh runs forward with his eyes glowing red.

CHAPTER FOURTEEN

"STONE GIANT!" GRALDOR IS moving too, following Vosh, hands reaching in his pockets while the troll moves with astonishing speed. I race after him, Damaris beside me, knowing I'm far too late to reach the elf and halfling in time, that the giant—the guardian of this bridge, obviously—has already crushed them against the stones and killed them both.

I underestimate Vosh's dexterity and speed as he bounds the last twenty feet, landing with both legs spread over our fallen friends, his powerful body swelling while he roars again.

But the stone giant looms over him, at least twice his size and I am now terrified for him more than I am for the elf and halfling.

Not to mention the state of the bridge. A selfish thought I can't suppress.

Fleur and Blossom are scrambling for safety, the pair on their feet and racing back toward us, turning as we reach them, the five of us able to do little but stare up at the two massive forms about to do battle on the narrow expanse over the bottomless chasm.

"Vosh!" Graldor reaches into his pocket and pulls out the statue's heart, but the troll growls in return.

"Run, you idiots!" He lunges forward, planting his shoulder in the gut of the stone giant. I back off half a step as the massive creature bellows in pain, his thick rock beard shedding a ripple of pebbles, deep set eyes flaring with red flames much like Vosh's. He's bigger than my friend but not as fast, not by a long shot, though when he swings forward with one arm, his fingers clip Vosh on the hip, sending him tumbling backward.

I leap over Vosh's shoulder, sword out, but as I stare up at the stone giant towering above me I realize I'm completely out of my league.

"Webb, just run!" Vosh is on his feet, hands grasping and tossing me back behind him. I land on my feet, barely, the others crowding around me, eyes locked on the giant as if they have no idea what to do next. Blossom is meeping soft breaths of anxiety, Fleur humming a low and terrified song while the dwarf beside me bounces on the balls of his feet like he wants to do something, anything. And Damaris stares.

"We won't leave you." I refuse to abandon Vosh, even if it means my death. The troll backs up two steps, forcing our retreat, while the stone giant lunges for him in slow motion, the sound of rock crushing at his movements sending dust and small pebbles raining down over us. Vosh grasps the hand that swings and jerks on it, the giant stumbling from the loss of balance, but quickly catches himself again.

"Get off the bridge now," the troll shouts over his shoulder. "I'll be right behind you."

"He'll just follow!" Blossom's protest is a wail of terror and she practically climbs my body, clinging to me. I sheath my sword and prop her on my hip. There's nothing I can do to fight, so carrying her isn't any trouble and brings me a small measure of usefulness.

"He can't." Again Vosh retreats and this time Fleur squeals an uncharacteristically harsh sound before skipping back almost to the end of the bridge. "Those carvings in his face. He's locked to this expanse. When we leave it, we're safe." I see them now, the etchings, realize those same carvings are in the archway that begins the bridge and have to believe Vosh knows what he's talking about. "Now get out of the way because I'm leaving!"

That's enough for me. I retreat as quickly as I can, unable to force myself to turn my back on the slow motion and yet inevitable feeling threat of the stone giant towering over us. There's an eerie sensation to the entire encounter because I know I'm moving faster than the hulking creature overhead and I'm positive I'm going to reach the end of the bridge before that massive fist descends fully and strikes the stones at my feet. And yet I'm unable to shake the surreal vibration of the moment as my boot exits the span and I'm back on the ledge, Blossom with her little face turned into my neck, arms twined around me, Damaris crushing me on the left, the dwarf on the right while Fleur scampers sideways as we sidle back the way we came.

Vosh doesn't leave, not yet, his bulk at the end of the bridge, and I know then as the giant's fist impacts the troll's upraised arms I may have just lost my friend for good. Instead, Vosh speaks a word in trollish, a powerful word with an echo like nothing else I've ever heard and the giant's fist slides sideways instead, impacting the curved arch of the bridge. Shattering it as it makes contact, shards of rock blasting outward in a volley of shrapnel that would have killed all of us were it aimed in our direction.

I can't remember dropping Blossom but I know I have because she's not in my arms anymore. I'm moving, faster than I've ever moved in my life, feet flying and yet I'm stuck in one place, heart pounding, stopping between one beat and the next, pained breath catching in my throat as I throw myself forward, hands outstretched. Grasping, reaching. Catching the thick belt of the troll as the bridge end explodes with the concussive force of the giant's descending fist and collapses down into the darkness.

Vosh wavers, dragging me with him and I'm falling but I will never, ever let go. But someone grasps my shoulders, catches my legs, holds me and heaves. No, not one person but many, hands using me to hold the falling troll as I hold him, the lot of us teetering on the edge of the precipice, the tumbling form of the giant disappearing into the black while I accept my death and embrace it when I heave on the massive form before me.

My feet slip, my hands cramp, and in the end I'm positive we're going over. But the tipping point shifts at last, the painful, terrifying instant of choice as if the Universe inhales and exhales and decides it's not our time after all. I stumble backward with the troll almost on top of me, the others crushed to the wall with groans and protests. And yet, it takes us a moment to separate, to shift away from each other and check ourselves for injury.

I look up from my own unscathed form and into the silent eyes of the troll who extends one large hand to pull me against his broad chest. Odd how I feel choked up and embarrassed at the same time, offering a halfhearted punch to his arm as he releases me and ducking my head so the others won't see me blush.

"My deepest thanks, Webb," Vosh says.

"I owed you that," I say.

CHAPTER FIFTEEN

IT TAKES US SOME time to gather ourselves, longer than I expect. Though when Blossom rises from where she's crouching and peeks over the edge near the remains of the bridge's shattered beginning, I'm not surprised she's the first to move.

"Now what do we do?" She points at the near end of the bridge, most of the front half missing. "We can't jump that far."

"And nor would we want to," Vosh says, voice soft and tired. "With the guardian gone, it's likely the rest of the bridge is unstable even for the lightest of feet."

"That leaves three doors or retreat back underground." Graldor grunts in unhappy irritation, glaring at the ground. "I don't like the idea of exploring this strange place further, but we don't have a choice, do we?"

"I have a guess as to the purpose of this place," Fleur says, "though it doesn't matter, really. Not while we remain trapped here."

"Let's split up this time," Damaris says. I'm not the only one who protests loudly and with nervous worry.

"We stay together," Vosh says, rumbling voice harsh around the edges. Is he, too, afraid? "I think we've proven unequivocally we're stronger together than apart."

Damaris seems frustrated, tsking softly into the darkness, fists on hips as she glares at the broken bridge end. "The queen doesn't have time for us to be cautious."

"Then I hope she has time to wait for others to take our place," I say, "because if we are foolish, we are dead and no help to her whatsoever."

She has nothing to say to that and I turn to the left and ignore her for the moment.

"Two doors that way," I say before spinning right. "And one in that direction."

"Let's get the single over with first," Graldor says. "Or, we could get lucky and find a way out."

I'm not convinced it's going to be that easy but I agree with his suggestion. "All for the path to the right?"

There's enough murmured agreement that I know we have a plan.

I turn to lead the way but Blossom is already skipping off like she didn't spend the last little while clinging to me out of terror. I hope I will find the kind of strength it must take to shift from utter fear to curiosity like she seems to possess, but my stomach still sits in knots in my gut while I pause and wait for Vosh.

He's hunched over the remains of the archway, his big hands cupped across one of the stumps of stone. I can hear him whispering in a guttural tongue but it's not before the column's base splits and a shining silver coin emerges I realize he's again speaking in trollish.

He straightens, the sparkling coin in his hand, turning to grimace at Graldor who opens his mouth as if to speak.

"Druid magic," the troll says, depositing the coin into his belt. "You have your own toys, wizard."

Graldor looks like he's going to argue and try to make a case before he shrugs and moves on, following the troll on the narrow path while I let the humor of the moment ease the last of my built up fear.

I'm the final one to reach the doorway, though it's not like being last is much of a detriment. A massive metal archway is sealed with a pair of matching doors. It appears to be copper to me, maybe brass, with what looks like the carving of a tree etched into it. But it's no ordinary tree, not full of leaves or thick with fruit. This tree seems to be stripped to the branches and twigs with the depiction of its foliage piled at the base of it like it's ill or in the throws of winter.

Fleur stands next to it, one hand hovering just above the metal surface, face twisted in concern. Graldor is whispering to himself, a faint glow around his hands giving him nothing, apparently, because he shakes his head at last and drops them to his sides, scowling. Even Vosh seems taken aback by the door, and Damaris glares like she wants to take her sword to it.

When Blossom springs forward to push against it, though, Fleur is faster, one hand on her chest, keeping her from touching it as the elf turns toward us all with a sick look on her face.

"There's something very wrong here," she says.

"Surprise, surprise." Blossom rolls her eyes. "This whole place is about as wrong as you can get."

"Can you open it, Fleur?" I lean closer myself, careful not to touch the metal, for a more detailed look at the carving. "Is this an elf thing?" I wince at my stumbling attempt at a question, but she doesn't take offense, too lost in the carving's lines and her own unrest to notice, I guess.

"I think so," she says. "Maybe we should check the other doors first, Webb. Look for a way out through them. I have a bad feeling we'll find no hope here."

"Oh, please." Blossom squeezes between us and before I can stop her, before Fleur can this time, the halfling presses both hands to the metal. "Let's find out what's back here, shall we?"

I open my mouth to protest, to tell her for someone who was just clinging to me and so terrified she couldn't act she might want to rediscover her inner coward, but there's no use, not anymore. Her touch triggers something that doesn't require an elf after all, and the metal groans, moans, the center of the door parting and swinging inward at her touch.

I hold very still at the exhale of fetid breath, as if someone on the other side is unhappy with our intrusion, though the scent passes and the silence from the tunnel beyond is absolute. Blossom seems taken aback by what she's done, either in regret at last of her hastiness or surprise her effort worked at all. It's Fleur who steps forward first, one hand raised, delicate fingers tracing over the air, creating a lighted pattern in the emptiness in front of her, a barrier only visible with contact reminding me far too much of the invisible wall we bypassed with the destruction of the statue. More than enough to raise goosebumps of premonition on my arms if I wasn't already worried thanks to Fleur's quiet hesitation.

"Shield," Graldor says, eager and apparently untouched by concern himself. "My job."

"No," the elf says in her musical voice, sadness there. "This is mine." She turns to look back at us. "This is powerful magic, dark and terrible. Elvish and forbidden to all who love the forest and the WorldMother."

Graldor's scowl turns to a grunt of surprise while Vosh sighs, deep and sad.

"Tree soul," the troll whispers like he's only now understanding what's going on. I'm still enough in the dark I almost ask but Fleur beats me to it.

"Indeed," she says. "Someone has taken the very life essence of an ancient oak and used it to form this shield." Her quiet unhappiness speaks volumes to me. Not just forbidden, but abhorrent as well. She doesn't move, her expression unchanged. "And so I repeat my previous statement. Perhaps we should leave this door alone."

"Something powerful hides on the other side," Graldor says, his tone alone a protest.

"Or is being held back," Fleur says. "A deathly danger that only the soul of an eld tree can contain. Are we willing to risk freeing such a threat for a chance at something we aren't even sure lies beyond?"

"Like an exit out of here?" Blossom sounds convinced.

"It could also mean an ally against the Demon King at the very least," Damaris says.

"Possibly to both." Fleur exhales in a breath that sounds like a breeze of first spring. "I cannot say for certain. Only that the casting of a containment such as this one can only mean whatever is held behind it is more powerful than we can possibly imagine."

"All the more reason to proceed," Graldor says. Even I hear the growing greed in his tone and it's not lost on Fleur.

She blinks slowly at him, her lean face alien in the darkness as shadows pool in her cheekbones, her eye sockets. "Your passion for more magic could lead us to our end, wizard."

"So be it," he says. "Are we here to wrest the Soulblade from the Demon King or not?" He turns, meets our eyes one at a time, no doubt in his. "If so, we're going to be needing a lot more to back us up than a few rusting hobgoblin swords and some stolen trinkets loaded with specific spells. We need allies."

"You mentioned dying wasn't the best use of our time," Damaris says to me, wry humor in her voice. "What say you, Webb? Worth it now?"

And then they are all looking at me like I'm the one who needs to make the final decision. Since when? I sigh, shrug. "I have a feeling whatever lies behind the other two doors on the far side of the cavern will offer about as much danger," I say. "And while I'd rather we were all in a tavern somewhere celebrating our victory, we're not. We're down here. And we need all the help we can get."

Fleur nods to me. "Agreed," she says. "Though I hope we're not fooling ourselves that this action we're about to take is a light one."

"Just open the barrier, elf," Graldor grumbles at her. "We have no choice."

We do, and yet he's right. Fleur must agree as she stated because she turns then and sings to the barrier, her fingers tracing a pattern over the air, light appearing and lingering where she draws out words in her language. I don't read elvish but I recognize its slow, sweeping curves and odd angles. Sparks sizzle, the light shifting from gold to green to dull ocher before it flares and fades away, only the last of her words written in the air lingering, the barrier's soft hum dissipating. And only then do I realize the sound was even there.

Fleur staggers briefly, the distant sound of a tree's leaves rustling as though in grief at its death. She hesitates a moment longer, one hand pressing to her chest, lips parted, tears trickling down her cheeks.

"This," she breathes, "is folly." And leads the way into the dark tunnel as if she'd never spoken.

CHAPTER SIXTEEN

WHATEVER HER FEARS, NOTHING untoward happens as we follow the elf into the tunnel, the darkness only ordinary shadows, the way narrow but not overly so and of the same hewn out stone as the rest of the place seems to be. I'm almost disappointed when nothing leaps at us, my tension having nowhere to go except to create a knotted pulsing at the back of my skull, a headache born of lack of action when my entire being believes it's necessary.

Vosh has to duck to enter, but he can move easily from side to side, taking up the last position while I step forward past Graldor and Blossom, past Damaris and to Fleur who seems withdrawn, anxious, both hands now clutched together before her, raised and pressed to her throat like she's choking on something she can't seem to comprehend or shake loose.

She pauses at the end of the tunnel, turning to face me, her glistening eyes huge in the low light. "So much pain," she whispers. "Agony and heartbreak. Death and despair unending."

I grasp her shoulders in my hands, trying to will calm into her through my touch. "Fleur, what's causing it?"

She shakes her head, looks away, blinking more tears. I follow where her eyes lead with my own gaze and realize, startled, the walls of the tunnel aren't stone entirely, but appear to have roots growing from them. Not just roots either. As I look up I see trunks of whole trees embedded in the rock, bark the same hue and blending into the rough surface. So easy to mistake them for stone themselves, their darkened trunks at level with the walls in places, though enough of them emerging it's apparent they're not carved but actual trees somehow appearing underground.

Blossom leaves us to touch one of them with tentative fingers, the wizard dwarf reaching out as if to stop her from doing so. It's hushed in this place, like a tomb of some kind, the air heavy and foreboding. And now, as I look around and absorb my surroundings, I know why I feel that way.

An entire forest is embedded in the walls and floor and ceiling of this place and their deaths have left an imprint on the stone. How they came to be here, how a full wood, more than likely once growing under sunlight, became trapped here with the bulk of their being lodged in rock I have no idea. Some foul spell, obviously. I'm not tied to trees the way Fleur obviously is, nor connected as the druid troll. But even I am not immune to the sorrow of such an act. Living beings should never suffer such a fate.

I emerge slowly, unable to stop my forward motion when morbid curiosity wakes, stepping from the head of the tunnel into a large, rounded room, leaving Fleur and the others behind, my boots crunching over the uneven ground. It's a forest floor under my feet, and yet it's not, the stone dominating, but enough twigs, moss and leaves on the surface to tell the tale. I swallow hard past the uneasy feeling of it, though the silence seems to be the worst, the empty quiet and stillness where life should play out. No rustling branches in the wind, no call of woodland creatures. Not even the hum of insects. Nothing. It's enough to break my heart.

Graldor pushes past me. If he's feeling the weight of what's been done here it's smothered by the determination on his bearded face, though I sense he's as unhappy as I am. "I feel power here," he says like that's all that matters.

I don't argue. That's not my purview, magic nothing to me whether I like it or not. I stay out of the way then as Vosh moves past me, step to one side and slowly circle the rounded walls, heading for the far side and the opening there. Another tunnel awaits, more silent, dead trees embedded in stone, more quiet, uncomfortable emptiness. Graldor marches down the tunnel and out of sight and Damaris, with a vague shrug for me as if in apology, goes after him. I join them, Blossom looking up at Fleur, holding the elf's hand as she leads her onward, Vosh circling the other way before joining us and walking with me at the back of the line.

"How horrid, this place," the troll says, rumbling quiet and for my ears only. "Wretched, whoever destroyed a forest of eld to make this tomb."

"But for what purpose?" I brush at a branch that touches my cheek, refraining from jumping when it does. But it's just a stray twig, not an attack. Tell that to my instincts that scream at me something is horribly, horribly wrong here and I need to turn around right now and run as fast as I can before whatever lives here comes for me.

"I can't say," the troll says. "But whatever the reason, Webb, it's a foul one and meant to bring suffering to those who visit here."

Was that the terrible power hiding behind the soul of the tree? This grim sense of foreboding growing stronger and stronger in my heart? Perhaps the spell is simply the means to crush the courage of anyone foolish enough to enter? I can only wish we could be that lucky. That is, until we emerge from the tunnel and Graldor hesitates. This new chamber has multiple tunnels leading away from it, a hub of some kind, the trees thicker here. Wait, is that whispering I hear? Not the others, no one is speaking. But I can swear I hear voices in the distance.

Don't I?

Graldor shakes visibly like a dog shedding water before crossing to the nearest exit and proceeding again while my mind twists and turns and asks why I'm here. I could turn around and go back, wait for the others to sort out this puzzle. Because I'm acutely in tune with the fact something is wrong beyond the dead trees or the worry Fleur has about what might inhabit this place that requires such protections.

Whatever she fears, whatever horrors we could possibly face, I am now utterly convinced we have been fooling ourselves we have any chance to escape this place alive.

And yet as we proceed nothing happens. Not one thing that threatens or increases our sense of dread. Though it does increase, there's no cause, no outward reason for it. The next chamber also has multiple exits and with a grunt of disgust the dwarf again takes the nearest one. I glance behind me almost constantly, positive someone is looking over my shoulder. And that's the only reason I come to fear something entirely different, beyond the possibility of attack. Because checking behind me reveals that the view hasn't changed as it should. That the trees I'm passing seem the same as the ones before, though that can't be true, can it? We've passed through three rooms now, three tunnels, all leading in different directions. So how can we possibly be passing the same trees?

I wait until Graldor marches into the next tunnel, focusing on what I'm seeing and fighting the dread within, enough it shakes off some of the oppressive fear and helps me regain attention to detail. So much so I'm positive when we exit the tunnel and enter a new one I'm seeing the same thing all over again.

This time when we emerge into a room, the same six doors available, I speak up. And when I do they all stop to turn and look at me, their expressions a mix of that same dread that plagues me, so at least I'm not the only one. Unimportant in the face of what I now know, though likely a big part of the whole problem. And one they need to understand.

"I don't know how we can be," I say, "but I think we're going in circles."

CHAPTER SEVENTEEN

I EXPECT AT LEAST one of them to scoff but Blossom nods instead, Fleur rubbing her upper arm with her free hand, the other still clasped firmly by the halfling.

"I've been thinking the same thing." The rogue releases the elf and scurries to the nearest tree. But, as her dagger hovers, instead of carving into the wood she chooses to hack at the rock next to it, her rusting blade digging a clearly visible X into the stone. She backs away, nods to it. "Let's find out if we're right."

No one argues when Graldor again chooses the way and it's not long before we emerge into a six exit room once more. I almost exhale in relief when I don't see Blossom's mark on the left hand wall by the first exit, but her squeal as she looks around, the fear on her face when she stops and stares off toward one of the other tunnels, makes my heart pound.

I follow her slowly, we all do, feet almost dragging on the forest floor in stone, as the halfling herself finds the energy to rush to the far wall and stops, pointing at the X mark she just carved in the room we left, the same room where we now stand.

Impossible. But my supposition has now been proven.

"This can't be." Graldor randomly selects a new exit and takes it, feet stomping beneath him. I go after him, to stop him, because I'm now positive he's just going to end up wasting his time. Apparently the others feel the same and when Graldor and I emerge from the tunnel's end alone, we're not. Because the rest of our companions are waiting for us on the opposite side of the room under the few branches of an oak tree that seem to have escaped the stone's embrace and hang limply over them like a canopy of despair.

"That answers that question," Vosh says.

"Impossible." The wizard spins around and looks back down the tunnel we just exited. It curves softly to the right, enough we can't see the far end, though I shiver as I realize if we could we'd likely see ourselves standing on the other side. I don't think that's something I'm willing to witness right now.

"Magic," Fleur says. "The eld trees are known for such deception when alive. Leading away those who mean them or their charges harm while guiding others they deem welcome."

Of course, I know the legends of such trees. I almost shake myself for not catching on, but wonder what it means for dead versions buried underground to have that power yet. "Elf magic?" That would explain a lot.

Fleur hesitates before sighing. "Yes," she says. "Though of my kind, impossible now that this forest has perished. At least, it should be."

Not comforting in the least and making me even more concerned about our present predicament. Surely living trees could be reasoned with, especially with an elf in our midst, her sub race's allegiance to them notwithstanding. But dead and unhappy trees infused with magic? This doesn't bode well.

"An endless maze," Vosh says then, speaking what I'm hesitant to consider or admit. "Perhaps we should return to the entrance and try to puzzle out this problem before we become lost?"

"That being where exactly?" Blossom has been skipping from tunnel to tunnel, marking each way with a different symbol. She's just finishing a deep Y in the bark of one of the trees while Fleur scowls at her. "What? They're dead, aren't they? And playing tricks on us." The halfling kicks the nearest root sticking from the wall. "Serves you right, tree."

There's no reaction for her impudence so either the tree doesn't care or we're in for far worse and they're biding their time. Which makes me shudder. "Are we trapped here?" That might be the foreboding I'm sensing. The whispering that's risen, is it the trees themselves? But they're dead? And yet, there is magic here. "Is that what we need to fear?"

"Wandering an endless maze of dead eld deep beneath the ground?" Vosh seems to consider that before sighing. "You may be right."

"No," Fleur says suddenly, shaking her head so hard her ear tips twitch. "There's more to it. More we need to be wary of." She hesitates then, like she has more to say, but her pinched face turns to the floor and she shakes her head as if refusing to consider what she's thinking. Or to speak it out loud. Instead, she says, "I just don't know what."

"Well, we can stand around and talk about it," Damaris says like she's finally reached her limit, dark eyes snapping anger, "or we can try to find a way out of here."

"This way." Blossom leads this time, down a tunnel and we follow as if in a trance, letting her take us into the dimness and then out again into the six tunneled chamber. Her markings are clearly visible and it's the first time I really accept we are trapped, that there's no exit this time. Returning to the entrance and the brass door is out of the question. Panic rises, my chest tight with it, though I refuse to show it and hope the others can't see how my hands shake as I clasp the hilt of my sword. What I'd give for the chance to swing it at someone, anyone, right about now.

Again she chooses, ticking off something on her fingers and again we follow, even Graldor appearing uncomfortable at last. Three more times the halfling decides on a path and three more times we go with her without question or complaint. And when we finally stop, the rogue turning to look up at us with her face creased in a frown, I know we're well and truly lost.

"I hate to be pessimistic," she says, "but I've just tried three of a massive number of options and none of them shows us the least bit of success." She tosses her head, topknot bouncing, freed bits curling around her pink cheeks now paled as she does her best to go on with her usual chipper tone. "Unless one of you can figure out the spell keeping us here," she says then, voicing my own fear, "we're trapped."

"I've been trying," Graldor says, hands wringing before him.

"As have I," the troll admits, head bowed. "My power can't reach past the trees. I should be able to talk to them if this is their doing. If they retain enough life to use their magic against us. But I just can't get through to them with their essence trapped in stone this way."

"I believe it's not the trees themselves we need to consider," Fleur says then, blurting her words as if forcing them past her lips. "I've already told you that."

"Then what, Fleur?" Damaris apparently turns to anger when she's afraid. I know how she feels and tap into my own frustration to give me courage. "What?"

The tall, slender ranger hugs herself. "I've been harboring a thought," she says, slowly, with agonizing anxiety behind them. "That the trees guard more than their own power. That they harbor in their tortured and trapped hearts the lost souls of elves."

I gape at her even as my entire being shudders. "What do you mean?"

She meets my eyes, misery there. "Buried in the cores of the eld, caught in the seeds of rebirth that can't be born thanks to the stone and the darkness." She drops her hands, turns in a slow circle. "Don't you know? Can't you feel it? This is no ordinary eld forest. This is an elvish burial wood, stolen from the surface and trapped under the earth where it doesn't belong. The worst possible prison for the perished echoes of passed elves." She shakes her head, sorrow a living thing that seems to compress her in on herself. "And we've walked into its endless agony."

CHAPTER EIGHTEEN

I'M STILL PROCESSING WHAT that might mean when Fleur's hands begin to glow.

"I can't keep this contained any longer," she says to no one in particular, her tears returning, making tracks down her narrow cheeks. "I must let it return to the place it belongs."

Graldor's face pales, Vosh lurching forward, both looking frightened enough by her statement and illuminated hands my own terror ratchets upwards. But neither has time to stop her, the elf's head falling back, her voice lifting in song that feels like a knife blade to my heart while light bursts from her in a rush of rustling leaves.

The glowing amber of the shield spell she absorbed turns green then a sickly gray before plunging toward the floor, cascading in leaf shapes toward the roots curving into the stone. They land softly, almost like fluffy snowflakes, drawn immediately inside with faint popping sounds, as if the tree roots suck them down, thirsty for more. Fleur sags as the last of the magic of the guardian tree's power leaves her, sinking to her knees in the middle of the floor.

"Fleur," Vosh's deep voice echoes with regret while he bends and lifts her into his hands, her slim form draped over his thick fingers. "These aren't the elves you think they are."

Graldor turns his back to us as the sound of sighing echoes from the six tunnel entrances, the dead trees now seeming to flex, their roots and branches moving ever so slightly. Enough I know I'm not imagining their wakefulness, their return to life, and there's nothing peaceful or kind or welcoming about this eld grove deep underground.

"I'm sorry," she whispers. "I had no choice."

I believe her, the oppression of this place only increasing and I wonder then how much weight she bore from the moment we entered, she of elvish blood. But it's clear as one of the trees wavers and a tall, slender form emerges, Vosh is right. These elves are nothing like the wood folk from whom Fleur hails.

If anything, the dark gray skin and black eyes of the ghostly figure tells of another branch of her race far less welcoming. When he bows his head to us, slim hands folded before the black robe he wears, faintly transparent but growing more substantial by the moment, I understand completely the overbearing pressure I've been feeling. Not just a cemetery grove, not just elves. But dark elves, born to chaos and hate and twisted by the magic they bear, the resting place of foul drow.

"Our thanks, fair one," his ghost speaks, for I have no doubt it's a spirit before us despite his continuing increase in visible substance. The whispering voices I've been hearing grow in volume, chatter now, excited and with purpose.

Though there's no joy in that purpose, I'm positive of it. "You have freed us at long last and our time to rise has come as we knew it would."

Fleur turns in Vosh's hands, one hand extending outward to the drow. "You tricked me," she says, sorrow in her voice.

"You answered the call of your blood," he says with a smile cruel enough to hurt. "Now pay the price for your kindness."

There's no further warning, no hint of any kind of threat aside from the continuing pressure of the despair that's been leaning so heavily on me. And then we're surrounded and being charged by more souls like his, drow appearing out of the floor in a rush of ghostly attack, from the ceiling, bursting from the walls.

My sword is of no use, I'm sure of that, but when I swing anyway, the blade in my hand in an automatic sweep of protection, the dark elf who hurtles toward me flinches and swerves, flying through the air and away again. The one that bursts from the floor at my feet cries out when my blade passes through him, though when his spirit parts before the metal it reforms again as he flees.

"They can't bear steel," I say, positive I've shouted that information, though in my head it feels more like I've whispered it. The others are already fighting, Fleur now on the floor in the middle of our group, only the weapons of metal we bear keeping the diving, swooping, charging figures of the drow ghosts at bay.

Something strikes me from behind and I stagger forward, falling to one knee, feeling my arm quiver and the breath leave my body a moment. Darkness floods my vision and I choke on my lack of air, clawing at my throat as something passes through me. I manage to swipe at the drow ghost and send her flying, shrieking her fury at my defense, but when I struggle to rise, I see the HW number on my embed has dropped by three points.

Graldor grunts beside me, almost topples over, recovers as I slash at the drow attacking him. There are so many, coming from all angles, it's impossible to defend completely. We might hold them off for a time, but I know my strength fades with each hit and that it's very likely Fleur was right from the beginning.

We won't be leaving this place alive.

The next time I fall, it's to both knees, my body flung forward as two drow attack from both sides, pulling through me and out again. I'm jerked face down, cheek impacting a tree root, stars sparking in my vision as my embed shivers.

"Webb!" I feel Vosh's big hand lift me, but he stumbles as he does, opening himself to attack in his attempt to save me and I'm dropped again, hitting harder this time. My arm sweeps out in front of me, trying to protect my face from the impending impact, and my sword strikes a tree, severing the root from the trunk.

Someone howls, a sound like I've never heard before, mournful and full of fury. Gasping, I push myself up to my knees and realize the attack has paused if only for a moment. The drow gather by the ceiling, their ghostly forms clouded by darkness, swirling like a vortex. And then they dive again, but too late.

I know their weakness now.

My sword cuts into the bark of the tree nearest me, the tip hitting stone but the blade embedding in the flesh of the eld oak. I don't have to tell my friends what to do next. They're already attacking the embedded forest as I am. The drow screams make my head ache, their swirling forms above us spinning faster and faster while I grimly hack apart the tree before me.

My blade finally severs the trunk, the top withering into ash in a slithering second, the tree that was dissolving and falling into a sad heap on the floor. The roots retreat while one of the drow explodes into tiny shards of mist before vanishing.

Another and another fall before us, the trees having no protection and the drow helpless to stop us, their power destroyed by our new knowledge. A few attempt to attack, but it's a weak effort that carries none of the strength they once used against us. My embed shivers once when I feel a drow slither through me, but I grimly carry on, knowing the only solution is the one that ends with the trees destroyed.

More and more of the spirits rupture, mist bursting into fragments that puff away to nothing. I finally look up, sweating and panting, my body aching from the effort, to find most of the trees in the space are gone, the floor now littered with ash, a few roots retreating and disappearing into the stone walls as if drawn away.

I'm not the only one who has stopped, though it's Fleur who is the surprising enthusiast, her short sword cutting away at the last tree, the final drow—our original greeter— swirling around her, weeping tears of black sludge down his narrow, ghostly face.

Save us. Barely a whisper now.

Her face set, she arches her back, sword held in both hands, and drives the point deep into the trunk of the last tree. I expect it to dissolve as the others had. None of us are prepared when it screams.

Fleur doesn't relent, grim expression making her look as ghostly as the drow that attacked, though I am forced to cover my ears with my hands, dropping my sword, my head feeling as though it might crack open from the sound. The others are in no better shape while the elf continues her slow and inexorable push, the blade in her hands sinking deeper and deeper, as if in slow motion, far into the trunk of the last tree.

When it finally dies, when the drow that circles explodes outward, the slithering ash cascades over Fleur, the sudden silence almost a blow in itself. I find I'm on my knees again, my hands shaking, something wet on my lip. When I touch my face, I pull back to find blood on my fingers from a nosebleed.

Fleur sways, her sword still in her hands, turning slowly to look at all of us. She appears translucent, as if she's used up everything she has in her attack, swaying slightly, elegantly, with the grace I expect from one of her kind, before she slowly topples to the floor.

CHAPTER NINETEEN

VOSH CATCHES HER IN time, just barely. He moves far slower than is typical for him and I know all of us have been affected by the battle with the drow, acutely aware we're lucky to be standing at all. Damaris's dark eyes are smudged beneath them, weariness on her pale face, her own nostrils streaming a flow of blood that's slowing to a trickle. Graldor shakes his head, finger in his ear, pulling out crimson. Blossom seems the least effected, though she's weeping and doesn't seem able to stop, little body shaking with silent sobs to the point I fear she'll collapse at any moment just like Fleur.

I check my embed, more out of reflex than curiosity, my head ringing from the lack of sound, the sudden quiet.

PH~11 ME~13 SP~11 EM~13 HW~18 BL~FH

"Stupid," Damaris says, voice cracking. "And lucky. But mostly stupid."

Blossom climbs to her feet, wiping at her face with both hands, snuffling as she does. She looks a fright, tears mingling with blood and her giant eyes blinking slowly as if she's waking from a terrible dream. But, despite my worries to the contrary and as usual, I'm discovering, she's the first to recover and when I watch her head for one of the tunnel entrances, I groan and rise and go after her. I can't let her explore alone, not now, though the feeling the worst is past us isn't lost on me.

No surprise to find five of the exits are now blocked off, a short distance from the beckoning of the false entries, just enough to create the illusion of a tunnel elsewhere. We've been led to the same doorway over and over by the magic of the drow and their horrible prison that was once a resting place. The final tunnel leads to the first room, the passage far shorter than it originally felt, no longer influenced by the maze magic. Blossom takes my hand absently, as if she's not aware she's doing it and I don't argue the point, welcoming the warmth of her fingers and the simple living contact, unashamed of the comfort her touch brings me.

We return to the others when we've established the truth, though both of us are silent, no need for words. When we join the others we find Fleur just waking, Vosh whispering over her as his power flows around her in golden light lit with edges of green, the soft sound of elves singing somewhere far in the distance and the thrum of the troll's voice beneath like the beat of some giant, earthy drum. I doubt he has the energy it to spare, and yet she looks terrible enough I know if I had the power I'd share it, too.

"They're gone," I say, unnecessarily, startled at the sound of my own voice. It's cracked and dull, as if the fight with the drow depleted it to a broken echo. I clear my throat, tasting the remains of the nosebleed in the back of my throat.

"Not all." Fleur opens one hand, shows me what she shelters there. I'm surprised to find she holds a tiny seedling in her palm, a single green leaf at the apex, slender white roots curling through the lines in her skin. "A gift from the tree, its death cleansed and soul free." Relief in her words, enough to make me feel a bit better about what we've done. Because regardless of the attack of the drow, the assault on their people, the theft and imprisonment of their resting place, that is the far greater affront. If I had been in their position, would I react any differently to someone who invaded my pain?

"That thing is an abomination." Graldor reaches for the tiny scrap of life, but Fleur's steady glare stops him in mid-grasp.

"Back off, wizard," Blossom snaps for her while I struggle to keep from slapping his hand away myself. "Let Fleur keep her tree."

I have no idea if it's a good plan or not to carry a seedling from the eld oaks we've just destroyed, but if Fleur wants it, I'm not going to fight her over it and, from the depth of feeling I see on the other's faces, we're all in agreement against the scowling dwarf. Only when Graldor backs off does the tension release, an anxious anger I hadn't realized I felt—and shared—until he did so.

We leave in silence, then, heads down, the weariness we all carry obvious in our quiet, a vague feeling of unease bordering on depression pulling at my heart. I've never been so tired, or felt so beaten and though I know we are, as Damaris said, lucky to be alive, I wonder if we have the fortitude to continue from here. Surely more horrors await us, possibly worse than this?

And yet, what choice have we? Going back to our cells is out of the question.

Fleur pauses at the exit while the rest of us step out onto the ledge. I wait with her, Blossom at my side, as the elf closes the door behind her. She sings to the etching of the tree in the metal and it seems to wake in answer to her voice, the dead branches sprouting leaves, fruit. She smiles at me, faint and sorrowful, before slipping past and joining the others while I shiver at the sight of the fresh oak tree now guarding emptiness.

There's nothing more to do but follow the others as they retrace our path toward the main tunnel, past the destroyed bridge. I'm about to suggest we retreat to the fountain room to regroup when someone laughs. The barking sound isn't coming from us, though. It echoes instead across the expanse, from the other side of the cavernous crevasse.

No need to tell the others to retreat. We seem to share the same mind as we tuck into the tunnel and the darkness, my ears straining to pick up further sounds. Something I don't have long to wait for.

"Idiot giant went and killed hisself." That grunting voice bounces toward us, distorted by echo and nearly unintelligible though I know instantly it's from the throat of another hobgoblin. More guards come to check on us? Likely.

"Dumbass giants and their stupidness." That's a second voice, joined by hissing barks that has to be hobgoblin laughter.

"Look who's talking, morons." I frown down at Blossom who winks at me, grinning. "Diverse vocabulary is not their strong suit."

"Hush." Vosh gently taps her on the top of the head with one fingertip. "Listen."

"Now how we meant to get from here to there?" Grumpy grunts of agreement greet that question. Either this cavern is a perfect sound conductor or the hobgoblins have zero sense of volume. Likely both.

"Search me," another says. "Oy! Figure of speech!"

More barking hisses. I strain to see them as I hear them but I just don't have the vision. Fleur and Blossom are both focused on something, though, as is Vosh, so at least some in our party are capable. I am surprised by my level of frustration and find my jaw aches from clenching as I strain to see despite myself.

"Them prisoners will starve," one says at last.

"Screw them," another growls. "What about me? I was hoping for halfling bones to crunch. Best marrow of all." The sucking noise that echoes makes Blossom's little face darken.

"Beasts," she snarls.

Their laughter is getting on my nerves.

"And our mates?" The voice doesn't sound too worried.

"Them bastards'll have yummy to eat," another says, regretful and grumpy.

"'Till they's starve to death," the first says with a hopeful upturn to its voice.

"Or the creepy critter statue eats them," another laughs.

Nice to see they cared so much for their fellow hobgoblins.

"Naught but to go upside," one says at last with faint regret. "Bosses will have a thought, methinks?"

"You thinks?" The second snorts. "Since when?"

They retreat, their barks and hisses and words fading to the point I can't hear them anymore, until we're in silence again aside from the faint sounds of our own existence.

"At least we have an answer, then," Damaris says. I can tell from her expression she's struggling to be optimistic at the discovery of our now clearly defined predicament. "There's no way across aside from the bridge." How she can remain focused while my heart sinks to my toes I have no idea.

"That those morons know of," Blossom says, patting her hand. I'm surprised by the halfling's emotional generosity but accept it personally despite the fact it's not aimed at me. I can use the encouragement right now. "Like they know anything."

Damaris tries to smile. "Agreed. And we're getting nowhere crouching here."

I want to suggest rest, food, water. It's apparent, though, from the mood of the others, the desperate reaching I feel in them for a scrap of Blossom's hopeful thinking—good to know it's not just me—that stopping now might mean more despair than it's worth. Instead, I trudge beside Damaris as she leads the way out and down the left side, heading for the next tunnel doorway and hoping we have what we need to survive another fight like the one we just fought.

CHAPTER TWENTY

THE NEXT TUNNEL FEELS far darker than the one we just left, stretching back into blackness with no door to pass through. The further one appears to have an archway as I lean out to check, though it's hard to see even that short distance with my human eyesight.

"One at a time." Damaris grasps Blossom by the back of her shirt and keeps her from her own curiosity. The halfling struggles faintly, little face turned toward the next tunnel as if exploring this one isn't enough for her.

"We might as well assess both," Blossom says, all innocent, twisting so fast she's out of the paladin's grasp before Damaris can nab her again. I always seem to be following the tiny thief and now is no exception as I walk in her footsteps, staying close while the others remain behind at the first entry.

Blossom beams up at me when she stops at the far door, like we're coconspirators and I'm on her side. If only she knew I'm here to make sure she doesn't get herself—or the rest of us—in trouble. The ledge goes beyond it by a few feet, but if the builders had planned to continue it all the way around to the other side and the far end of the bridge, they either lost interest or time. I can almost see from here where the bridge ends, the vague form of darkness and faint illumination a tunnel exit that the hobgoblins likely used to leave. So close and yet far enough away there's nothing to be done about it.

The halfling is already examining the giant iron door, a massive padlock hanging like a pendulum from the far right hand side. "Want me to pick it?" There's far too much eagerness in her, little fingers probing it with the length of wire that started all this before I can stop her, but I hook her around the waist and lift her into my arms to stop her from completing her work.

"Not yet," I say. She wriggles in my grasp a moment then sighs heavily and falls still, arms crossing over her chest while she dangles in my arms. "Patience for once?"

"I hate waiting." She's pouting when she turns her head enough for me to see her expression, so young in appearance while I wonder if I've been assuming as much. She's a halfling after all. They have long lifespans and are notorious for their youthful faces far into middle age. Still, there's a feeling of buoyant childishness in her that screams teenager I find hard to ignore.

"And I hate dying." I set her on her feet again, looking up at the towering single door. It's not rusted or pitted at all, looks brand new, large rivets holding it in place, massive hinges larger than Vosh's fingers bolting it to the archway.

"You're being ridiculous and a scaredy cat." The halfling doesn't try again, though, joining me as I turn back to return to the others.

"So leaving a big, unknown door unlocked behind us as we explore the first tunnel of unknown threat is a good idea, you think?" She glances up at me and winks and I laugh because I can't help it. Her seemingly endless access to joy is infectious and welcome despite the dire circumstances. I can use the chuckle, to be honest. "Now who's being ridiculous?"

The lightened mood she's granted me falters when we stop next to the others who stare into the black tunnel they seem reluctant to approach with growing apprehension. I can feel it from them, in the tension in the air, and I wonder if it's worth it to explore.

"We know there's no exit here," I say, keeping my voice as quiet as possible.

"That the hobgoblins know of," Blossom corrects me.

"And there may be magic here we can use to escape," Graldor says. Not quite an admonishment of my hesitation, but close.

"Oh, for goodness sake." Blossom darts ahead and into the tunnel mouth, turning to glare at us with her hands on her hips. "Are we going or not?"

My stomach tightening once again, reluctance triggering my frustration, I shrug and go after her while the embed in my arm quivers.

I'm almost instantly engulfed in darkness so deep I can't make out anything. Not Blossom who I know is just a few feet ahead of me or Damaris I'm positive strides beside me or even my own hand in front of my face when I lift it to check. The embed in my arm is silent now, the glow from the letters and numbers absent and I find my feet slowing, progress falling off, hands now out in front of me as fear I'll walk into something becomes a real danger.

"Blossom." I feel my words die, swallowed by the black.

"Here, Webb." Something bumps into my legs, hands on my thighs. I can barely hear her, as if she's talking from a long distance away. "Where is everyone? Can you see?"

The fact she can't makes me even more nervous. "Fleur?" I half turn toward where I last remember seeing the elf and someone impacts my left shoulder, the barest of pressure following as I hear the ranger's voice in my ear.

"I can't see anything," she says.

"Nor I." Someone grasps my belt, a thick hand when I touch the fingers, and the voice is Graldor's, though as distant as the others.

"Any idea what this is?" Damaris's words seem to burrow into my ear and I feel the barest touch on my skin. Is she that close? It's impossible to tell.

"Whatever the cause of the darkness," Vosh's deep voice vibrates in the black, the looming feeling of him nowhere to be found, though I know he's there with us somewhere, "it apparently makes it impossible for us to go further."

"We can't just turn around without finding out what's in here?" Blossom's protest is high pitched and cuts through the shadow.

"Without the power to penetrate the darkness, there's not much we can do." Damaris sounds like she's losing hope at last and I wish there is something I can do to bring back her drive to push on. But there is no way forward here. Not when one step could lead to a plummeting fall or some other danger we can't perceive in the black.

Not to mention the fact I'm certain there's more to this darkness than just devouring silence and shadow.

"Fine then," the halfling sighs. "I guess you're right."

"Maybe we should take each other's hands as we retreat?" Vosh's big one touches my shoulder, pinching ever so lightly. "So no one is lost."

Someone's slips into my left, feels like Fleur's slim fingers. And on the right the rougher warmth of Damaris. Blossom's touch disappears and I hope she's found someone's hand to cling to.

"Everyone secured?" Vosh sounds more like a kindly teacher leading an unruly group of children than a powerful troll druid. I grin shakily into the darkness, the growing sense that something is watching us only fed by all that inky shadow. And yet, I still shudder as we turn as one, murmurs of agreement equaling the six of us, Vosh once in the rear now leading the way back toward the entrance.

I draw a breath to exhale a sigh of relief just as that air is stolen from my lips and crushing weight grasps me in an embrace that feels like death.

CHAPTER TWENTY~ONE

I'M POSITIVE IT'S OVER, that we're dead and this entire experience is my last. That I should have pushed harder to stop this exploration, should have done something. The embed in my arm twitches, the faintest red light appearing in my peripheral vision and a woman's voice—that voice from the white light that started all this— says, "*Terminate Soulblade Stage?*"

"No!" I gasp that word even as light flares around me and I can breathe all of a sudden. My chest heaves, heart pounding, and I choke while I cough and air returns to my lungs. The world sways but I'm okay and I recover quickly enough, finding the others standing around me, doing the same to varying degrees. Just an ordinary stone tunnel now, like all the rest. The darkness is gone, but where?

And then I realize we're all looking around, in shock and fear. All but Graldor. The dwarf stands with his back to us, shoulders rigid, the darkness spread out before him, filling the tunnel past his upraised arm. I ease forward, gaping as I realize he's holding the rune stone from the prison below and that sweat trickles down his temples while his eyes flicker to the side, meet mine.

"Hurry," he whispers. "I can't hold it for long."

It's not an organized or orderly retreat. Vosh lifts Blossom in one hand and scoops Fleur in the other, spinning and running for the end of the tunnel not so far away as I expected but feeling like it's going to take forever to get there. Damaris hesitates but I shoo her off, pausing with Graldor who takes a slow and painfully shuddering step backward.

"Can I help?" I know I can't. I can only stare into the dark that waits on the other side of the fragile power the wizard holds in his hand. The rune stone pulses, the light in it growing faint as if draining the heartbeat out of the magic it contains.

Graldor doesn't respond, taking another agonizing step back. I reach for him, to lift and carry him as Vosh did for the others, but he shakes his head abruptly.

"Disturb me not," he says. "I'm barely hanging onto this as it is, Webb." He licks his lips with slow deliberation. "Go. Save yourself."

"Never." I flinch as he retreats another step, the darkness oozing closer. Tendrils reach for the tips of Graldor's fingers, sucking at his flesh. He blanches, a faint grunt of pain emerging from his lips and I look frantically back and forth from him to the exit and know there is absolutely no way he will make it.

Not on his own.

"Do your best to hold it," I say and, before he can protest further, I grasp him around the waist and leap for the end of the tunnel.

The darkness devours both of us, pulling at my legs, my hips, my waist. I'm scrambling to escape, the dwarf wizard writhing in my grasp, the rune stone's power just enough to keep us from being swallowed all together while I lurch to a slow battle mere feet from the exit, feeling as if I'm being sucked down into a pit of living quicksand.

Graldor is up to his neck, my arm deep in the black, the dwarf muttering spells that do nothing against the darkness. It climbs to my chest, my neck and as I strain to keep my chin out of the slithering shadow, a massive hand reaches toward me and grasps me firmly, pulling on me with the kind of tearing pressure that warns I'm about to be shorn in half.

The precipice of death looms yet again as my bones and muscles strain within the confines of my skin. I can feel my eyes bulging, my breath long gone from my chest, the darkness eating me alive. And then, with an abrupt popping sound, I'm free, flying forward with the wizard still in my grip, impacting Vosh's chest so hard he staggers back and almost falls over the edge of the path.

Damaris grasps me by the arm, pulls me back as the rebound of being popped like a cork under pressure makes my head ache. I land hard on the ground, the dwarf beneath me, but when I roll free of him he groans, opens his eyes, meets my gaze.

"Well done," he says before his eyes roll into the back of his head and he passes out.

I stare up at the troll who bends over me before struggling to sit up, staring into the darkness in the tunnel, shuddering as I see it undulate briefly against the entrance. It finally retreats into its lair to await another victim foolish enough to risk its embrace.

This fool is done, for now.

I don't have to suggest we rest. My HW stands at nine, a frightening number that sends a chill down my spine. We've strung ourselves out to the edge of our limits and, when the weary troll retreats down the path toward the tunnel leading below I go with him. At least there is still food, though it's not the delicious banquet we'd first seen. It's already begun to rot, as though the spell that made it no longer sustains it. And the beds that first looked so appealing and welcoming are crumbling, the blankets moldering with mildew and damp. Not that we care. The water remains cold, fresh, clean. I drink my fill, eat enough that's not yet spoiled to satiate my empty stomach and make a bed next to the wall with my arms for a pillow. Because I'm tired enough to call that comfort.

When I wake, it's abruptly, to the shudder of my embed and with a curse at my laxness. Except there's nothing that can harm us anymore, as far as I know, the guards unable to reach us. The others sleep as I've been doing, Vosh's snoring sounding like a bellows firing a massive hearth. Blossom is curled in his lap where he sleeps sitting up against the wall, Fleur leaning delicately against his side. Damaris lies flat like the dead, though the rise and fall of her chest tells me she's all right.

I glance at my embed and note my HW has returned to the high teens, climbing slowly as I observe. I need more sleep, will do so when someone else wakes, but for now I need to watch over the others.

It's only when I sigh and prop myself against the wall to do so I realize one of our number is missing. And, with my heart in my throat and my hand on my sword, I force my weary body upward and go looking for Graldor.

CHAPTER TWENTY~TWO

I FIND HIM EASILY, though it takes a bit of searching and by the time I stand next to him outside the tunnel of the black devouring whatever it is that tried to eat us, I'm tired again. He doesn't acknowledge I'm there for a long time, hands clasped behind his back, beard jutting forward as he simply stares into the undulating darkness on the other side of whatever barrier keeps it from consuming us.

Probably a good thing we didn't manage to destroy the protections that hold it to that tunnel. The only sort of good thing we've stumbled over in the last little while.

He startles me when he finally speaks. I'm about ready to turn and leave him, to let him have his contemplation in silence. But just as I've gathered enough energy to walk away, the wizard's deep voice reaches me with low, sad words.

"The rune stone is dead." He shows it to me, held in the palm of his hand like a broken toy he's asking me to fix. "I drained the last of its magic shielding us."

I don't comment, not sure what he wants me to say.

He's not done, staring down at it before he tosses it into the darkness before us. The misty black undulates as it passes, and then falls still again. I almost ask him why he did that when he speaks again. "Is this what I've become, then?" I wasn't expecting a question and don't know how to answer, but apparently it's meant to be rhetorical because he doesn't wait for a response before he goes on. "Is this what my teachers have made me? No." Graldor shakes his head, staring at the ground now, instead of the shadows. "No, I take full blame for greed and the drive for power bringing me to this place and this circumstance."

While I tend to agree with him—we're all here for our own reasons and no one has forced us to come, though I of all of us might have the best case to argue if it came to that—my compassion won't let him carry such an accusation without argument.

"It's the nature of power to call to power," I say. "We're all guilty of wanting more, Graldor."

He squints up at me like I'm not doing a very good job comforting him. "You're a good soul, Webb, with a valiant heart and wisdom beyond the years you seem to have lived." When he sighs his beard ruffles from the exhale. "A fighter's desires, though, are for a longer, stronger sword, better armor, more muscles. Maybe a bit of magic embedded in a shield or breastplate to keep one safe." I nod, uncomfortable but agreeing because he's right. "But a wizard, Webb. A wizard's life is about acquisition of magic. As much and as often and with as little remorse as possible."

I doubt that very much. "You're hardly evil incarnate, my friend."

Graldor grunts. "That's the first time in many moons anyone has called me friend. So you be the judge if you've read me right or wrong."

He's got a point. "So standing here in the face of your near death has given you insight you've previously been missing, I take it?"

Graldor laughs at that, slaps his hands on his curving belly. "Clever boy," he says, "for a human." Again with the sighing, but this time he seems to use it to shed some of his melancholy. "I could have taken another road, you know. My father's offer to inherit his place as the lord of our tribe still stands. And were I a wizard of lesser power I might have shed this drive I feel for magic and sat that seat with his axe in my hands."

"Sounds like a rather boring life," I say.

"Indeed. Though there's enough goblins and orcs and other creatures in the underearth to fight I'd have lived a good enough existence if I'd not passed that down to my brother." Graldor drops his hands to his sides, tilts his head as he stares again at the dark, though with curiosity on his face now rather than sorrow. "Arrogance has a power to it, too, I think. Bolsters courage. But there's weakness in it I'm only beginning to understand."

His humility makes me uncomfortable and I find myself clearing my throat as the intimacy of the conversation brings a flush to my cheeks.

I'm spared trying to find words to share when Damaris joins us out of the dimness, appearing almost like a ghost, and speaks while I shudder at her unexpected arrival. "There's nothing wrong with knowing what you want and that you're capable of having it," she says.

"No," Graldor says, "but there's a limit that leads you and the people you're with to the brink of destruction once too often." He turns and bows slowly to us both, face solemn. "Your forgiveness for my impatience. I knew in my heart entering that place," he tilts his chin toward the dark tunnel, "would lead to hardship. As I did the elvish cavern. And yet, the feeling of magic within was irresistible to me."

"Was, you say," Damaris murmurs. "No longer?"

Graldor shrugs and grins suddenly, an open, happy expression I've never seen on his face before. It makes him look younger, less wise and yet much more content.

"No promises, paladin." He laughs then, gestures for us to return to the fountain.

I let him pass, Damaris lingering and together we watch him go.

"Sad to see him lose his nerve," she says.

Startled, I turn to her. "I disagree," I say, offended for him by her attitude, wondering how she missed the point entirely. "Is he not learning caution and care are just as important as power?" Maybe I'm losing my nerve, too?

She wrinkles her nose at me. "Honestly, Webb," she says, striding off, voice echoing back to me, "you're like no fighter I've ever met."

Which makes me pause and think a moment. About Graldor's two paths, how that feels like it reflects on me. Ponder the truth of who I might really be. Am I the fighter Damaris pegs me, that I assume I am due to my weapon skills and lack of anything magical? Or is there more to me, to my being here in this time and place, to the embed and the woman's voice and everything I can't seem to remember?

She offered me a way out. When death was imminent, that voice gave me the chance to end this and I knew to say no. Or was that the right decision? Who was I to possess the power to rewrite my own timeline?

I can stand here for eternity, I realize, and uncover nothing further. And, with a faint shudder, I glance sideways into the tunnel, suddenly far less comfortable being here alone with the swirling, eddying darkness that seems to taunt me as I step away and follow the paladin and wizard back to the others.

The answers are out there. I will find them. For now, I will do my best to protect those I now call friends while trying to escape this place. The bigger truth can wait.

CHAPTER TWENTY~THREE

THE OTHERS ARE AWAKE when I return, already sorting through the last of the food that's even remotely edible. I manage a hunk of bread that's fairly clear of mold and a small slab of what smells like salted ham enough I risk it, the round, orange fruit I peel when I'm done unfortunately rotten to the center and inedible.

I discard it in disgust and return to the fountain to rinse my hands and drink deeply, two scoops of clear coldness doing wonders to restore and refresh me. My HW level has reached twenty again, so I'm grateful for the rest, but we have another door to check and, ultimately, a chasm to find a way across if we hope to leave this place and not die of old age here.

A chilling thought, though age will likely not be our fate if the lack of food we're now facing is any indication. I'd rather not slowly starve if I have options and have to be honest I'm more likely to end up troll dinner if it comes to survival of the fittest. Vosh might be a thoughtful druid with the kind of intelligence that makes me wonder about his past but I've seen who he can be and refuse to contemplate the inevitable should it come to a fight between us.

I'm not the only reluctant one to finally rise from the fountain's broken edge and face the tunnel exit. Despite her talk of lost nerve, even Damaris seems hesitant, though Blossom finally heaves one of her characteristic sighs and eye rolls at us before trudging off without her usual spunk toward the chasm. I think that just makes me feel worse.

Fear has become a familiar friend so I'm not as knotted in my gut, however, when we pass the watching darkness and its tunnel prison, each of us skirting it with visible unease, and reach the iron door. Despite all we've been through, or perhaps because of it, my anxiety is far less than I'm expecting. Vosh examines the final barrier while the rest of us wait for him to complete his visual and then magical check. Graldor does nothing to interfere, and I wonder if he's still thinking about what we discussed. More than likely.

The troll steps back from the door, just enough room on the ledge for him to do so. "I've been thinking about this place," he says. "And the more we explore, the more I'm positive this is a prison."

"We figured that out," Blossom says with her usual sarcasm.

Vosh grins down at her. "I'm not just talking about *our* prison, halfling."

She frowns then while I nod, Fleur sighing softly in her musical voice.

"As I suspected," she says.

"I've been thinking the same thing," I say. "These aren't traps meant for us to find, to keep us from escaping."

"Agreed," Vosh says. "They are more likely just more prison cells that have been designed to contain what we've been rather foolishly setting loose."

I shudder as I look over my shoulder at the tunnel we've passed, hoping he's not referring to it. "So this door we plan to open, it's a cell designed for whatever's on the other side?"

Vosh doesn't answer, big face turned back toward the door.

"More than that," Fleur speaks up. "I believe this entire cavern is just a level, one of many. That below and above us are other prisons we can't reach."

I hadn't considered that. No surprise Blossom spins and sinks to her knees at the edge, lying on her belly to dangle over and look down. "You're right!" She sounds excited though I don't think such exuberance is a good choice right now. Still, seeing her return to her bubbly excitement is a happy relief. "I can see other tunnels and ledges." She flips over, looks up, careless in her haste, fearless while my heart sits in my mouth with the need to save her from herself. "More up there, too! Though I think there's a ceiling in the distance. Another bridge, maybe two. Vosh, you're so smart." She winks at him despite it being Fleur's suggestion of the layers before her head bobs back again while she continues her examination.

Vosh carefully plucks the halfling from the edge and sets her on her feet safely away from where she could fall. "And so, it's more than likely this doorway will not lead us to another exit but to a dead end, much as the rest."

Damaris grunts, face tight with anger, protesting with her whole body as she seems to twitch in denial. "We can't just stay here," she snarls.

"No," he says. "We can't. And yet, I'm only speaking what I know is true, Damaris. We must be aware of what we're walking into."

She still looks like she's ready for a fight, but she doesn't say anything.

"So what, then?" Blossom glances around at all of us. "Do we turn and leave? Go drown our sorrows in the fountain, toss ourselves over the edge in despair?" I snort at her bright tone mixed with the hideous suggestions she throws out so lightly. "Cut each other to pieces, lock ourselves away once more down below?" She spins in a pirouette, stopping with her eyes locked on the metal entry that is our last hope. "Or do we open the damned lock and see what the Demon King thinks deserves a prison cell with such a fancy door?"

When she's done, she's staring up at me as if waiting for something and I finally nod when I realize what she wants.

"Open it," I say.

Despite her shift back toward her usual mood, even her intense curiosity seems blunted as she reaches for the lock and, with clever, quick fingers, opens it with some elaborate gesture that's equally subtle and indecipherable to me. I rub my eyes and shake my head. I'm clearly not a thief, then. Nor a magic user either, I realize, when the lock falls away and Vosh, his deep, smooth voice rumbling, speaks a soft word to the metal door.

It swings open just a bit, enough to let light from the other side wash over our feet. At least it's not more darkness lying in wait for us. I take that as an excellent sign, though when I take a step forward, Damaris beside me, I hear Blossom whisper, "The light you see at the end of the tunnel..."

My mind finishes her thought with a quiver of concern I crush heartlessly. It's highly unlikely there's a dragon down this corridor. At least, I tell myself so as I prod the edge of the door.

It swings open, thudding softly against the interior wall, the hinges perfect and silent, as if newly made or oiled recently. Why does that make me feel worse and not better? I exchange a quick look with Damaris who shrugs and strides through, shoulders squared and I follow her, knowing I'm as guilty of arrogance and ego as Graldor.

CHAPTER TWENTY~FOUR

WE DON'T HAVE FAR to explore before we're stopped at a stone wall. I look around at the tunnel, about as ordinary as the others we've explored, while Blossom crosses her arms over her chest and glares at the short end of this one.

"Now what?" She kicks at the stone under her feet, irritation amusing if we weren't in a precarious situation. Though it appears we're not under any kind of threat that we can see or sense.

"Go back?" Fleur's musical voice sounds disappointed, too. Her big eyes blink in the dimness while she hugs herself with her long, slim arms, something she seems to do frequently. What comfort does it bring her? "Perhaps this particular prison has as yet to be stocked with its resident."

But Vosh seems confused, shaking his big head. "There's something wrong here," he says, though without real concern so I'm not nervous. His curiosity seems to push him forward, past Blossom who grumps as she steps out of the way. I follow and watch when he lifts one massive hand. "The tunnel feels longer than it looks, if that makes any sense?"

I shake my head, despite the fact he's not looking in my direction. I find myself gaping a moment later when his fingers brush against the end wall—and disappear.

"A shield of some kind?" Damaris has slipped herself in beside him, too, tucked under his lifted arm.

"No," he whispers, with a hint of awe. "Not in the way you mean." He extends one big hand, palm up, and a gap the width of his touch appears beneath it.

I peek through the hole, close enough to see tiny fragments cascading past his fingers. "Sand," I say, touching it briefly. It feels warm, like the sun has been heating it, though more likely it's the magic keeping it mobile and the friction of the pieces rushing past each other that's creating the sensation.

Vosh nods. "Sand." He drops his hand again. "Some kind of curtain creating a false image of a solid wall where none exists."

"Not a very good protection for whatever lies beyond it." Blossom is at least less grumpy and more interested now. She slides around me and looks up at the troll. "Path, please?"

He shrugs and holds out both hands this time, raising his arms high enough I can see easily into the gap and the tunnel beyond the curtain of sand. I'm beside Blossom when she trots through, though I have a firm grasp on her arm as she tries to race on ahead.

"Wait for the others," I say.

She wrinkles her little nose at me, clearly irritated. "I'm tired of all this waiting," she says, jerking free of my grasp. "You have fun doing more of it and I'll go see what's ahead."

She bounds away before I can stop her and I have to bite back a massive sigh while Damaris joins me.

"Halflings," she says.

"Rogue halflings." I shrug. "You're right. She's going to get herself killed."

"Then at least we'll know what the threat is." Damaris grins and slaps my shoulder, her good humor just taking the edge off her words. I know she doesn't mean it and that Damaris is frustrated. We all are. But I still take offense despite myself and feel my back stiffen at the suggestion.

"We'd better catch up with her." I stride down the tunnel, Graldor grumbling behind me, Fleur's softly musical voice answering him though I'm too angry suddenly to make out what they are saying. What's triggered my temper? It's not until I exit the tunnel at stomping speed, feet whispering through sand coating the floor of the long, rectangular chamber at the other end, I realize what's wrong.

I feel responsible for these people, though I barely know them. Blossom waves at me from across the room where she's examining a doorway, locked to her entry. Not like that's going to hold her back or anything. The tension in me eases the moment I see her again and my arm vibrates. I don't have to look down to see the BL and FH are glowing white. I feel the faithful hero of my beliefs in my bones. Like it or not, the small group of adventurers I've taken up with are now a part of me I won't easily shed.

"Nice of you to join me." Blossom winks and the door she's been lock picking swings open as she pushes it with flourish, grainy wood silent on metal hinges. "Care to take a peek?"

I circle the edge of the room, Damaris caught up with me, the others in tow. I don't feel entirely comfortable until I reach the halfling thief and peer around the corner of the door with her.

There's light inside, faint and glowing, enough to reveal this place is some kind of storehouse for clothing and boots. Someone has piled them up in the center of the small space, a mountain of cloaks, tunics, breeches and leather boots, shoes and other incidental items.

"I could use a change," Blossom says, sniffing at her sleeve before darting within and climbing the pile, pulling out things before discarding them again.

"How uninspired," Damaris says, droll humor remaining, apparently. She enters behind the halfling, her feet hissing through the sand on the floor. I look down, the thick stuff barely at the edge of my boots, though it feels heavier than I expected. Fleur glides past, Graldor, too and Vosh last, leaving me alone in the main room to watch the thief toss random items at various members of our party.

"Webb, catch!" She balls and heaves a tunic at me, the thick fabric soft under my hands when her excellent aim almost hits me in the chest. I have to admit, it will be nice to have something new to wear. The clothes I presently own are threadbare and dirty.

I strip off the horrible remains of the hobgoblin chainmail and then my shirt, knowing I must reek of rust. It's not cold in here, but I'm feeling exposed and goosebumps rise when I shed the thin protection I've been wearing. I quickly pulling the tunic over my chest, though when the halfling offers me new breeches I shake my head, same for a cloak. I feel no need for extras, anxiety slowly rising again though there's no hint of a threat here. Boots, on the other hand... I finally give in and join the others in the small room, finding a tall pair in brown leather, much heavier and more comfortable than my own, and when I do depart for the main chamber my feet are happy.

I could try the lock on the next door myself, but Blossom, now decked out in layers of clothes in so many hues I wonder if I'll go blind from the glaring mix just looking at her, bobs past me and dives for the lock. She grunts when it opens easily and doesn't wait for me, exploring on her own while I fight the urge to pull her back.

"This is more like it." Damaris's growling pleasure turns her into a stalking hunter while she brushes past my shoulder and into the room. Identical to the last, this one houses a towering pile of armor. All kinds of breastplates and chain mail, greaves and helmets, shields and even swords and other categories of weapons all tumble together in a large heap of shining metals of all kinds.

"Am I the only one who finds this odd?" I have to admit I'm tempted sorely by the sight of new chainmail and the thought of replacing the nasty stuff I bear now has a large appeal. But where has this stockpile come from? And why is it here?

"Not at all," Graldor says, hefting a silver axe that makes him look more dwarfish fighter than wizard. "This is a prison, isn't it? And I don't know about all of you, but the things I had with me when I arrived weren't in my cell for me to use against the guards."

That does make sense. My feet shuffle over the sighing sand as I cave and join them, sorting out a lovely, sparkling shirt of tightly woven links. I toss the hobgoblin's rusting disaster aside where it sinks partially into a small pile of sand in one corner and don the new mail. It falls to my knees, lighter than I expected, while Fleur drifts to me, fingers tracing over the links.

"Excellent choice," she says. "Elvish mail will serve you well."

I run a hand over it, surprised how soft it feels, almost like fabric, covering my upper arms to my elbows. My arm shivers and I push back the cuff of my new tunic to glance at my embed. The PH and the number beneath glow white as my original thirteen turns to fourteen, strength increased thanks to my new acquisition. Interesting. I feel rejuvenated, like I've had more sleep and maybe a week off with good food and lots of rest. A sheath and new sword, long and sharp, hang from a thick belt around my waist and I help myself at last to a lovely round shield that makes me feel much more secure.

A quick return to the first room and I'm fully equipped, gloves and even a belt pouch to grace my hip. I'm grinning like this is some kind of game or entertainment, turn to join the others while Blossom tackles door number three. And notice with a slow return of nerves the sand on the floor now touches the toe tips of my boots.

Has it risen? But no, I had other boots on before this. Surely I'm mistaken. I glance around, looking down at the floor, bend to lift a handful and let it fall between my fingers. It's just sand.

And yet, I'm now uncomfortable all over again and hurry across the center room as the others disappear into the third doorway, to the sound of Graldor laughing.

One peek inside is all it takes to tell me why he's happy. I've never seen such a collection of potions, scrolls, staves, wands and other magical items—I can only imagine they all contain magic—in my life.

"A treasure trove beyond belief," Vosh breathes. "And now I'm with Webb. Are we certain there's nothing off about this?"

"Oh, hush, would you?" Graldor dives into the pile, his reticence about his hunger for magic clearly slain by the promise of so much power right in front of him. And, as I watch the troll sway, I know he's about to give in, too.

And who am I to stop him?

"That's it." Blossom sounds disappointed now, fingering the fabric of the top layer of tunic she wears. Does she really need three? A thick necklace of gold and gems bounces around her neck, wound around several times and I wonder where she dug up the prize. I haven't seen trace of coins or any other treasure aside from the security of the sword and mail I now wear.

"That's enough," Damaris says, seeming much happier in a breastplate over her surcoat, massive sword strapped to her back. She looks the part of a paladin now. "Hopefully, with our replacement armaments and these two with access to who knows what magic we can find a way across that broken bridge."

"Aren't you the optimist." Blossom sounds far more sour than I expected. "This is too easy."

So even she is feeling what I've been fighting since we entered here.

"Then perhaps we should hurry." I look up, find Graldor has been stuffing things into his clothes, that Vosh holds a massive staff in both hands. "You two find anything we can use to escape?"

The wizard grunts at me. "You warriors, you have no idea. This isn't as easy as picking up a blade and a mail shirt, Webb. It'll take us time to sort out what's here and what's usable."

Vosh looks guilty as he nods. "Agreed."

I chew my bottom lip, looking down. And notice what I've been fearing all along. That the sand I've been telling myself isn't rising has now covered the toe of my boot and we've been complacent too long.

Punctuated by the sound of Fleur screaming.

CHAPTER TWENTY~FIVE

I SPIN AND RUN before I can think, feet sticky in the sand, feeling myself slip and slide on the now shifting footing as I turn around and hurtle back into the main room. Fleur is nowhere to be seen. I throw myself toward the second door and find her standing back from the pile of armor, her face tight with shock, a newly strung longbow and quiver of arrows over one shoulder and something white and long in one hand.

When I come to her side and take it from her, her horror reverberating between us, made worse when I examine the length of light, white material and realize with a burn of bile in the back of my throat it's a bone.

"Elvish," she says, pointing at the end and the rounded joint end where a spiral of pale green winds around it as if a vine grew inside at one point. "My own sub race."

I weigh the bone in my hand and, from the slimness and feather light feel I can only assume she knows what she's talking about. Damaris has joined us, takes it from me and looks closely, before offering it to Fleur again. The elf ranger shakes her head and backs away, wiping at her long, narrow nose with the back of her hand.

"There's something wrong with this place," she says. Meets my eyes with her own still caught in the grief and disgust of her discovery. "We need to leave."

I'm in full agreement with her and have been feeling the same thing though I can tell from the frown on Damaris's face she's going to argue. I don't give her a chance, offering my hand to Fleur.

"We can wait for the others outside," I say.

The ranger nods, a slow, deliberate motion, though she ignores my offer of a hand to hold and brushes past Damaris, on her way to the door. I've offended her without trying to, have to remember she's not as frail as she appears. This sense of protectiveness can be a detriment. Why did I think the powerful ranger would ever need me to support her?

The paladin rolls her eyes at me but I'm not letting her get away with her attitude this time.

"You're as bad as Graldor when it comes to being driven by something," I say, knowing I sound harsh and hurtful and not caring despite the buzz in my embed, the itching where BL is tattooed. "She's right and you're treating this like we haven't encountered anything to fear so far. Just a reminder—we have. And this feels far too good to be true."

Damaris's jaw tightens as she glares back at me. "Don't you think I'm aware of that?" She tilts her chin at me, eyes roving over my person as she speaks. "I don't see you discarding what you've taken from this place, Webb, so don't be a hypocrite. We need what the wizard and druid can find if we're going to escape and you know it."

"Maybe," I say. "And maybe we're just putting ourselves in needless risk by poking our noses in where they aren't welcome." This feels wrong and yet right at the same time. My embed buzzes again and I glance down at it, surprised to find it's gone a moment before blinking twice and returning. I shake my head, feel an ache starting between my eyes as a wave of dizziness washes over me.

It's gone as fast as it appeared, though I worry more when it fades. What triggered it and why am I suddenly feeling like I shouldn't have said anything, that Fleur is being sensitive and Damaris is right?

I look down a moment to gather my thoughts, the paladin stomping off. Or trying to, her boots swishing through the sand, now up to her ankles. And Fleur's horror is my horror for a totally different reason. Because as I look back to my own boots and realize the risen sand has now covered my feet as well, a sure sign of something I've been ignoring since we arrived, I bump an object beneath the surface with my toe when I lift my foot to shake free of the clinging stuff and dislodge something white.

Something rounded with two deep sockets where eyes used to be, to slits where nostrils fed air into lungs, a jawline with teeth that grin at me as if this entire thing is a hilarious joke the skull is only now letting me in on.

I bend, lift it from the sand, turn the face toward me. "Damaris."

She's at the door, tsks as she turns back despite her obvious irritation. And freezes when I rotate my hand and show her what I found.

Shock turns to a flash of worry and then to regret, all in a rapid flicker over her face. "Maybe Fleur is right after all," she says. "I'll get the others."

I leave the skull behind, setting it carefully on an upturned breastplate though I want to throw it across the room to get it away from me. Slowly, carefully, heart pounding, I do my best not to run for the door, the sucking sand now pulling at my boots. I stumble as I near the exit, over something big that crunches under my heel when I step down. A ribcage and sternum surface, the sand disgorging it in my path and when I bend over to stare down at it I see the sand isn't rising.

It's moving. Shifting. Swirling, cycling over itself in an endless dance of particles that has far less stone in it than I first thought. Much too white to be made from the rock of this place.

I shiver from that thought and stand upright. Definitely time to go.

I almost run into Vosh as I exit, the big troll hurrying toward me. He pauses, massive feet deep in the sand, gray stone face paled out to near transparency.

"I think we made an error," he says. "This isn't a stockpile, Webb."

I nod, grim and struggling with the need to just run, run as fast as I can and get out of this place. "I know," I say, thinking of the white flecks, the way the stuff moves, how it's not entirely rock and blurt what I'm now afraid is truth. "I think it's a graveyard."

"The sand." Blossom swallows hard as she joins us, Vosh lifting her into his hand to get her out of the sticky stuff. "It's not real sand, is it?"

I don't want to answer because I know if I voice what I'm thinking—if I actually put words to the guess that this is the remnants of people we're walking in—I'll start screaming and might lose my mind.

Instead, I shake my head and turn to the main exit, Graldor, Fleur and Damaris all standing in my way.

Their frozen state makes my stomach quiver and I approach them slowly, heart pounding while the sand—bits of bone and remnants of the owners of the things we've taken—swirls and eddies around my lower calves.

I stop, frozen by shock, when I pass Damaris's left shoulder and look toward the center of the room. And the vortex of rising sand that hisses as it begins to turn, faster and faster.

Even as I feel the stuff beneath my boots, surrounding my feet and ankles, start to tug me forward, toward the slowly opening maw forming in the middle of the room.

CHAPTER TWENTY~SIX

I'M NOT AWARE OF Blossom until she leans past me and tosses something into the sand. I watch, horror only growing by the moment, when the small bit of cloth she threw begins a slow and yet inexorable journey to the center of the vortex.

Not one of us moves or even seems to breathe while the scrap of fabric finally makes the final turn and disappears into the middle of the circling sand, popping under as if swallowed, the steady hissing of the particles rubbing against each other growing louder. I look down and find I'm up to my calves at last, and rising, the pulling of the swirling matter making it harder to stay upright.

"Time to go," Damaris says.

"Any ideas to that end?" I glance toward the first door we entered, see that the sand churns at the foot of it.

"Circle around and fast," Blossom says, already moving. I nab her in time to keep her from doing something stupid, handing her firmly to Vosh who cups her in his grip, fingers spread. She peers between them like they are prison bars, glaring at me.

"I don't think that's an option." I take a page from her book, lifting free the small pouch I took, still empty, and throw it to the threshold of door number one. It's devoured immediately, surfaces briefly three quarters of the way to the center of the vortex and then appears one last time, a moment later, just before being swallowed like her offering.

"That answers that," I say. "Any magic in that third room that might give us an advantage over sand that wants to eat us?"

"Not sand," Fleur whispers but I'm not going there, not letting my mind even think about it despite knowing what I'm sure I know.

"Nothing." Graldor's growling tone isn't comforting. "Mostly healing spells and a few weapons. A growth spell. I'd need more time to go through it all."

"And, supposedly," Vosh says as if this is merely a curiosity and not life threatening, "should the original owner of said magic had access surely they would have escaped themselves and not left anything useful behind."

That wasn't helping.

Blossom wriggles through the troll's fingers and he lets her out to stand on his palm, but only because, it seems, they've come to some kind of agreement she won't attempt escape. She hefts a small knife in one hand and throws it with intent, right to the center of the vortex. Gone in a flash. She then points to the weapon room and she and Vosh lumber on his large legs—much more stable than her tiny body in the rush of sand—to the door, vanishing inside. Only to emerge a moment later, the knife in her hand.

"At least we know where we'll end up if that gets us." Damaris scowled at the vortex as if unafraid and not realizing what the whole issue is.

"Our clothes and weapons and magic, you mean," Graldor says. Even he's pale now, and looks down at the sand up to his knees with growing concern. "Sorted efficiently by item. But what about the rest of us?"

"Bones." Fleur shudders, hands cupping her elbows. "Just bones left."

Damaris opens her mouth, frowning, like she's about to argue before her cheeks turn white and she hops to the right.

"Something," she says in a low, shaking voice, "just bit my foot."

I open my mouth to ask her what, though it's possible I'm also going to yell at the top of my lungs for us all to run instead of voicing a simple question. But I choke on my breath that's meant to fuel my words and my world tapers to a narrow, dark tunnel with a writhing, sucker laden tentacle dangling into view at the end.

Damaris must see the expression on my face and realize it doesn't mean anything good because she spins with her sword clearing the sheath on her back, just missing clipping my shoulder, and lets out a hoarse shout at the sight. Her blade takes the tip off the reaching wriggler and it retreats as the sand's hissing grows in volume. But even as hers vanishes into the ceiling—now a spinning mass of moving sand, too, as are the walls, and how did we miss this?—I hear Graldor grunt and Fleur scream again.

More tentacles, grasping at us from under, from over, from the walls themselves, lurching out of the sand to wrap around wrists, elbows, clasp at clothing with sticky round suckers. My entire body shudders in utter revulsion as I cut free a tentacle. It's strong but not impossibly so, the suckers undulating as they fall free into the sand. It's the sheer number of them that make panic grow in my heart, the way they lunge and retreat as they are cut, only to be replaced by three or four more.

I cleave through a handful at once, the dark brown scaly substance and pale beige suckers washing out to the tone of the sand as they impact the ground and disappear under the swirling stuff. I'm over my knees in it now and I know it won't be long from the pressure of its turning toward the center of the room I have minutes if that before I'm swept off my feet.

And the tentacles aren't helping, obviously part of this creature's—if it is a creature—hunting strategy.

I hear Graldor speaking in dwarfish, see magic flying from his hands, but nothing seems to work.

"Webb!" He meets my eyes. "We need a bridge!"

Well, yes, I know that already. Until I realize what he means. "You want to go over it?" Over the center of the vortex. He's lost his mind. But I latch onto the final spell he mentioned and have a spark of a thought.

"It's the only way." I spin on Fleur and grasp for her belt pouch. She's fighting off a tentacle and isn't fast enough to stop me when I retrieve the sapling from her possession. The remains of the eld forest cemetery is slightly bent but still green and, when I turn back, Graldor is waiting for me, as if knowing exactly what I have in mind. I toss it into the air in front of the wizard who catches it deftly before turning to the druid. "Vosh! Make it grow!"

The bulky troll doesn't hesitate, trusting or understanding, either one. He cries out in his language, his words sending out a shockwave in visible ripples, hammering all of us with the thudding passing of its power. I dodge a tentacle and slice it in two before looking down to make sure I'm in one piece, only to shout and leap out of the way of the suddenly growing tree that's hurtling toward me.

"It won't have anywhere to root for long," Vosh says. "Get on and go, now!"

I see instantly this insane plan has a chance to work. The root ends of the tree are embedded in the wall, the canopy surging toward the other side of the room—across the surface of the vortex. Tentacles are dropping already, testing the tree as it continues to grow. Vosh heaves the protesting Fleur up and onto the trunk, Blossom after her, gesturing for Damaris to go next. She does, forcing the elf and halfling to keep moving while Graldor boosts up with help from the troll and scrambles to follow.

I'm next, though I pause long enough to help Vosh free himself from a tangle of tentacles that have wrapped around his thick legs and arms, trying to pin him down. It's as if the creature has chosen to take out the largest of us, or sees him as the biggest threat. Or the tastiest snack.

"Go." I point for him to leave. "I'll guard your back."

"I need to keep the tree alive." Vosh hesitates. "You can't do that."

"The tree won't last much longer," I say. "Either we run now," I cut apart three tentacles before glaring at the reticent troll, "or we're dinner."

"Agreed." Vosh leaps up on the tree and runs, though he has to duck low to avoid the ceiling, tentacles immediately dropping to engulf him. I'm after him, cutting as carefully as I can, see Damaris has turned back and is helping from her end. The tree groans beneath us, sagging in the middle of its trunk. We have moments before it collapses, I'm positive of that and, even as my mind makes that determination, I hear cracking and turn back to see the roots are pulling free of the sand on the far wall.

"Just go!" I push against Vosh who, free enough at last, makes a massive leap, shaking the tree violently with his exodus. I hear him land but don't see him past the dark green leaves dominating the other end of the bridge he's made from Fleur's sapling. Damaris waves me on and spins to run and I follow, but not before something thick and heavy wraps around my ankle. I trip, falling on my face, bruising my cheek and sending stars into my vision. My sword slips from my fingers, but I catch it at the last moment, heaving the point up and over the bark of the tree while I half flip over and slash at the tentacle.

It's massive, like the creature is pouring all of what it has left into a final push attack. It must know its meal is about to escape. A quick slice and it's severed and I'm scrambling across the trunk, the oddest feeling, sideways instead of up, throwing myself into the canopy.

Big troll hands fish me out and drag me forward, away from the leaves rustling violently when the tree groans again, like a living thing that suffers as it dies. I stand with my friends, their eyes as big as mine, as one giant tentacle rises from the vortex and grasps the tree around its middle, cracking it with a giant rapport before dragging the entire oak down into the sand.

Someone's hand grasps my arm and turns me around, pushes firmly between my shoulder blades. I'm running then, as I knew I would have to, eventually. Graldor yells something magical at the wall at the end of the tunnel and I realize, as the floor beneath me shifts and heaves, the entire place we are fleeing is the inside of some kind of creature.

Power from the dwarf explodes outward, shattering the sand wall. I leap for the other side and safety, Damaris beside me, Blossom rolling into a little ball as she tumbles. I flip over before I slide to a halt and see Vosh escape last, Fleur on her knees, as the sand wall snaps shut and turns to stone.

"How could you?" Fleur leaps on me and pummels me with her fists, fury on her face, tears running down her lean, pale cheeks. I don't even bother to try to fight her off, taking the blows as punishment. I know I've broken her heart to save us, as much as my taunting of Vosh brought out the troll in him. I'd stolen the seedling gift that meant so much to her.

It takes Vosh lifting her clear, gently pinning her with one big hand, before she stops fighting.

"You wanted to die, ranger?" The dwarf spits out sand and I want to throw up knowing what he had in his mouth was nothing like crushed stone. "Is that it?"

"You sacrificed a sacred rest eld oak," she snarls at me, ignoring the wizard, sounding nothing of her musical self. "You arrogant, pig headed, vile human."

"He saved us," Damaris says, voice low and deep and rough. "Fleur, he had no choice."

"There's always a choice." She turns her head away. "Put me down, druid. Who dares call himself such."

"I wish there had been an alternative, Fleur," Vosh says, his own voice full of regret. "The tree's sacrifice will always be remembered."

Blossom hesitates, meets my eyes. Then sighs and goes to Fleur who won't look at anyone. The halfling grasps her hand and places something in it. When the elf does check, she lets out a low, moaning cry before hugging the thief who sighs and lets her.

"I was going to keep it as a surprise for later," Blossom says. "You're welcome."

Before we can ask, Fleur lets her go and opens her hand. Showing us the tiny acorn inside.

"Well done, halfling," Vosh murmurs.

CHAPTER TWENTY~SEVEN

FLEUR MAKES AN ATTEMPT to apologize to me a moment later, her lean face pale, hands shaking. I wave it off with a head shake and a weary smile.

"Please know how sorry I am," I say, beating her to it.

She hesitates before rushing toward me, cool lips pressing to my cheek. "Thank you," she says, turning immediately away. "For saving our lives."

I had no idea elves were so volatile, but under the circumstances I'm feeling a little torn in a million directions emotionally myself. My arm vibrates and, when I check, the EM number flashes white before falling still, BL remaining the eternal faithful hero.

Someone, whoever gave me this embed, thinks I'm doing all right.

Graldor, meanwhile, has turned toward the broken bridge with a growing grin on his face.

"Think it might work, Vosh?" He looks up at the druid who shrugs his big shoulders.

"Worth trying, I think," the troll says. "The heart can handle it?"

"Only one way to find out." Graldor rubs his hands together, looking far too pleased with himself for my liking.

"Mind filling us in on what's made you two so happy?" Damaris doesn't need to sound so peevish. We survived yet another horror, and this time with benefits we can all be happy about. Even Fleur who murmurs a soft song to the acorn before she tucks it into her tunic. Likely to protect it from grabbing hands. And from the expression on her face, anyone who tries to take it from her will end up pitched over the side of the chasm, no questions asked.

"Come with us and let's find out." The wizard and druid leave us there, heads together—quite a sight for a towering troll and blocky dwarf, but they manage. I follow, all the tension easing out of me, and try not to think about the sand in my boots. First chance I get, they are coming off.

The pair in the lead don't stop until they reach the end of the bridge, the archway's broken off curve too close to the edge for comfort. But, it's there Vosh stands, one hand on the top of the shattered column, while Graldor turns to the rest of us.

"We're pretty sure we have the means to cross," he says. Flinches. "Have had it all along."

I didn't need to hear that.

"It's a joint effort," Vosh says with a grin. "And only came to us because of our ordeal. So perhaps we can be forgiven for missing the obvious."

I'm willing but only because we're all present, alive and in one piece.

Fleur's hand goes immediately to her breast. "You're not touching this tree," she says in a flare of protectiveness that strips all the music from her voice.

"I don't need it," Graldor grumbles, some of his good humor gone again. He clears his throat, stomps one foot, and when he goes on he sounds less like a giddy child and just grumpy again. "You're welcome, by the way."

"Get over it, you two," Damaris snaps. "Just tell us what you have planned and exactly what 'pretty sure' means?"

Vosh laughs, deep and rumbling, just loud enough to echo, an eerie sound in the quiet dimness of the chasm below. "What he means," the troll says, "is the wizard believes between the two of us we have the means to grow rock."

"The tree gave me the idea," Graldor rushes on as if Vosh's share returned him to his place of happiness. "If our combined powers could make a tree sprout, surely a troll's ties to stone could do the same for the bridge. Using the heart of the statue and its devouring power, we take rock from here," he pointed at the walls around us, "and put it there." Again he gestured, this time at the bridge.

"In theory," Vosh says. "Untested."

Graldor grunts. "As of yet. But you're about to do something about that, yes?"

"Ready when you are." Vosh nods to the broken archway.

"Wait." Damaris takes a step back. "Is this going to be loud or...?"

"Possibly," Vosh says, glancing at Graldor. "And maybe a bit dangerous?"

"Like, define a bit," Blossom scowls back and forth between them.

"Earthquake? Rock slide? Utter collapse?" Graldor sighs. "We honestly have no idea."

The others hesitate, though as I see it this is a silly conversation. And finally say as much. "Can we go back?"

Everyone shakes their heads.

"Can any of you fly and have kept that little tidbit to yourselves?"

A smirk and a punch from Blossom, more headshakes.

"Then fix the stupid bridge," I say. "We've run out of dumb things to challenge for no reason and without information we need to stay alive."

Damaris barks a laugh. "You heard him."

In the end, it's rather anticlimactic, though no small feat and, in hindsight, a beautiful thing to behold. Graldor offers his hand to Vosh who takes it, engulfing the dwarf's up to his elbow in his thick fingers. The wizard cups the stone heart in his free hand, holding it between them. And then, without further ado, the druid begins to hum.

My knees vibrate with the sound, tingle starting in my feet and traveling up to my hips, into my gut. I clamp my lips together to keep my teeth from chattering but the shaking settles after only a moment, the faintest sound of the crack of stone breaking on the other side all that I can hear aside from Vosh's low voice.

"It's working." Fleur ghosts to the edge of the bridge landing, peering into the dimness. "How remarkable."

Blossom bounces on her toes before rubbing at her upper arms and then her cheeks. "Hurry up already," she says. "I've got the all over tickles from whatever you're doing."

Vosh doesn't answer or seem to change his speed. The volume of his voice remains the same, head bowed, Graldor silent beside him.

Even I can see the stone now, arching toward us, though it's thin, about as tall and as wide across as one of my feet is long. It's going to make for precarious walking. Still, its soft landing and attachment on this side end in an exhale from the troll and a deep, shaking sigh from Graldor. When the wizard tips his hand, the stone heart of the statue crumbles into dust and cascades from his palm, used up.

"A shame," he says. "But effective."

I'm about to suggest a rest before we move on when Blossom, her face twisted into a cheery grin, dances out into the expanse before turning to wave at us. "Come on then, you slow pokes," she says. "Time's a wasting!"

Fleur follows her, delicate feet silent on the stone. I gesture to Damaris who goes after them and wait for Graldor and Vosh myself. The wizard sags, shakes his head. When he looks up to meet my eyes, his are full of weariness but a particular kind of peace that makes me smile.

"Well done," I say.

"Thank you." He pats Vosh's hand. "A pleasure working with you, druid brother."

"And you, wizard kin," Vosh says.

Graldor bows to both of us before surveying their creation. "A bit thin."

"Best we could do," Vosh says. "Are you going to keep poking holes in it or cross it?"

The dwarf grumbles something before hitching his belt and easing out across the narrow span. He wavers, halts a few times. But, by the time he's lost to the dimness I'm sure he's reached the thicker end and will be fine.

"Your turn, friend Webb." Vosh's big eyes are too quiet, his soft smile too gentle.

"I think you're going first," I say. "And I think we both know it's far too narrow and light for my weight." The troll sighs then, sits. "You cross and I'll rest. When you reach the other side, let me know. I may try to thicken it further then. After a short nap."

"I'm not leaving you here." He should know that by now.

Vosh opens his mouth, protest ready. And then he laughs and embraces me. He's a rock, literally, huge body like hugging a boulder. But I can hear his heartbeat and when he releases me the warmth of his stone skin has chased off some of the chill in the air.

"Fine then, stubborn fighter," Vosh says. "We'll die together, if that's your choice."

"If that's the will of whoever looks down on us," I say. "Now move it."

I'm positive the moment he puts his full weight on the rock it's going to go and I'll be swept down into the chasm behind him. Because I meant what I said and I'm on his heels, right at his back, as he steps out.

The stone sighs, I'm positive of it. But it holds. And, as he sets another foot out, balancing over the darkness, I find myself grinning like I've lost my mind.

It's slow and painful, that trip across the bridge he made. And there's two or three moments I know he's going over, that he's lost his tightrope balance and can't possibly hold on. And then we're stepping out onto the original bridge, the cobbled way arching toward the other side.

My breath catches when I hear stone cracking, and I leap forward, Vosh at my side, when the stone finally releases its strength and caves in. I land hard on my hip, the troll at my side, and watch this end of the bridge collapse into the chasm and vanish.

"By the way," Vosh says to no one in particular with a slight catch to his voice. "Forgot to mention, that poor tree wouldn't have survived, Fleur. No more than the bridge did. Speeding the growth creates momentum all the way to the other end of the life cycle."

"Excellent to know," Fleur murmurs in the quiet. "I'll remember that."

CHAPTER TWENTY~EIGHT

WE REST FOR A short time, not long enough, really. But we're all too wound up after making it across the chasm finally to sit still for long. Even Vosh, as weary as he seems, is up and peering into the tunnel now visible to all of us at the top of the sharply rising path that leads from the head of the bridge.

Light flickers from the dimness, torches in the distance, more than likely. And guards. I feel like I've switched modes, from explorer to fighter yet again and though it's true I should be more afraid of what I'm about to face, I'm actually less concerned than I should be. But, at least the hobgoblins and other soldiers the Demon King must have guarding his citadel are known enemies, combatable and killable. What we're leaving behind us?

I'm happy to be on this side of the chasm. And striding side-by-side with Damaris, our swords out and ready, the others tightly packed behind us, the tall and imposing troll druid taking up the last of the line. I glance back, saying a silent farewell to the subterranean prison we've escaped against all odds, feeling optimistic and almost light when I turn again.

It's a climb up the winding path, narrow but smooth compared to the rest of the rocky floor, carved into the stone and leading in only one direction. The tunnel we enter is much taller and wider than the ones we've left behind, and the light up ahead is clearer now, the pinpoints of torches flickering and beckoning us onward. There's no sign of guards, something I almost regret. A good fight with something I can swing at without wondering if I can actually defeat my foe would do wonders for my confidence. Still, I'm focused and tense, thighs burning from the climb, the scent of wood smoke and food drifting toward me as I pass the threshold of the tunnel.

"Careful," Damaris says, barely a whisper. I glance at her, surprised to find she's frowning.

"You, being cautious?" I almost snort at her but hold back my derision. She doesn't deserve it and we've come through too much together for me to let it get between us. "Since when?"

She shrugs, giant sword balanced in both hands like it's a toy. "Just be ready for a fight."

I almost comment she doesn't need to coach me, this isn't my first battle or adventure. But the moment my mind registers that snarky comeback it stutters and freezes, my entire body seizing for a single heartbeat as everything goes dark—

—*galloping over a vast field with an army at my back, the heavy lance in one hand, six foot shield in the other while the plate mail pushes me deeper into the saddle*—

—*leaping from the side of a mountain onto the back of a shining dragon who carries me into the sky*—

—diving deep under the ocean with a gold trident clutched in one hand, a ball of glowing fire in the other—

—prowling a ruined city with a heavy P90 automatic rifle grasped in both gloved hands, my night vision goggles too tight against my sockets while something moves in the distance—

—clinging to a silver bulkhead, one hand clamped over the cut in my suit, precious oxygen leaking out as my blaster drifts off into the darkness of space—

—and then I'm walking up the tunnel, a short stagger hitching my step while I inhale sharply and feel my entire body tingle in time with the vibration in my embed.

Damaris glances at me, frowning. "What's wrong?"

I stare at her a moment, not sure what to say, no idea what just happened but knowing it's nothing she can help me with. I can't remember everything, but clearly I'm starting to recall some of what I've lost. But do I want to? And what does it all mean?

It felt real, as real as this advance down the tunnel, as the people at my side, my back. There's no question I'm not losing my mind—I tell myself so—not when every single memory is as crisp and clear as if I was just there, on that horse, in that city, hanging from that space ship. I shouldn't know what a blaster is, what a gun can do. And yet, I'm positive if someone dropped one into my hands I could field strip a handgun in under twenty seconds.

It's disorienting and yet comforting, too. I'm finally remembering who I am. But who I am seems disjointed and out of connection with who I thought I was. Funny, it should bother me more, shouldn't it?

And then we're reaching the torches and there's no more time for thinking or memories, not when we pass into the light and come to a halt at the base of a set of spiral stairs heading both sharply down, deeper into the prison as well as upward into the ceiling.

Narrow spiral stairs. I purposely don't look at Vosh, don't focus on the fact he's too big and there's no way he'll fit. Because he's going to fit and I'm not leaving him behind even if that means we have to find another route or make the stairs bigger. By force, if necessary.

The troll doesn't seem concerned, passing me on his big, quiet feet, touching the staircase's stone curve with one hand. "This is our exit," he says in that mild voice. "From what I'm feeling, this stone is the core of the citadel and travels not only deep into the prison here but all the way to the top of the Demon King's tower."

"Just like that," Graldor grumbles. "Easy, then."

Vosh nods, smiles down at his friend. "Just like that." He glances back at the stairs. "A long way to go yet. But the end is in reach."

Blossom goes first, bobbing upward and around the first bend, the solid side of the staircase almost taller than her so we only see the bouncing tip of her topknot as she goes. Fleur follows, Damaris on her heels, the two handed broadsword she carries back in its sheath, no use to her in tight quarters. Graldor is, as I'm discovering, next and leaves me with Vosh, our now well accustomed order.

"Don't worry," the troll chuckles. "I'm not going to argue this time. I'll manage."

"And I'll follow," I say. "You first, master druid."

Vosh squeezes into the narrow way, ducking his head, shoulders tight against the walls. The spiral widens slightly as we go, but he's still moving in increments, grunting softly while he pushes against the immobile sides of the staircase. Still, we're making progress, and it's not long before we reach the others, Fleur peeking around Vosh's hip to meet my eyes.

"Hatch," she whispers.

I nod, wait as the sound of air sighing and a breath of food and smoke is borne down the steps over me. My stomach growls in discomfort but I ignore it, waiting for word of what's ahead. There's nothing I can do back here but guard our rear, after all. I almost fret over not being able to see, but there's no way I'm squeezing past Vosh under the circumstances.

It's only a moment later when Blossom scoots down the steps around the troll's foot and to my side, Damaris crouching with Graldor and

Fleur to peer through the gap at the troll's hip as the thief fills us in.

"Good news and bad news," she says, looking back and forth between me and Vosh.

"Good news first, little one," the troll says.

"You were right about the exit." She smiles brightly before that happiness fades and she slumps slightly. "Bad news now. The hatch leads out. Into a big room." She shrugs. "Full of guards."

CHAPTER TWENTY~NINE

BEFORE ANY OF US can say anything to that, she perks again. "I'm going to sneak in though and see if I can distract them." Like she already had this plan in mind before she even came down here to talk to me.

"You've lost your mind," I say. "What do you expect to do, just waltz in there and sit down for dinner?" Yes, my stomach is definitely interested in those food smells despite my efforts otherwise.

She winks at me. "Silly, I don't ask for anything, you should know that by now."

"It's too dangerous," Vosh says while Damaris shrugs.

"I think she should go," the paladin says while my arm embed twinges and the BL letters glow faintly red. The hero in me struggles against the need to keep the halfling safe from all threats. Ridiculous under the circumstances, and yet a part of me as much as the embed in my arm. "She has the best chance of sneaking around up there. If we try a frontal assault, we're done."

"And there's an excellent chance someone's going to come to the hatch shortly and head for one of the other prison levels." Graldor is right, of course. "We don't have time to debate."

"Either we attack," Damaris says, "or Blossom tries to find a way to clear the room."

I hate the thought, my arm aching as I hover on the edge of an argument. Until the halfling rogue leans in and grasps my hand and smiles up at me in her sunny way.

"I can do this," she whispers. "Let me do this, Webb."

My embed falls still, the white glow returning and going dark. I nod to her then to the others. "Blossom's going," I say, hoping it's not the last time I see her alive.

I hear the hatch crack, smell the food again, feel the waft of air coming down toward me before it's cut off and I'm left to stand there, feet shuffling from moment to impatient moment, palm sweating on the hilt of my sword. It's impossible to control my growing anxiety as the seconds tick by, imagining the little halfling being captured, tortured, killed. And I let her go. Did nothing to stop her.

Vosh's deep voice rumbles around me as he leans closer, big face almost touching the top of my head as he speaks. "She's going to be all right," he says. "She knows what she's doing."

I nod. "I should have gone with her."

"And gotten in her way and made a mess and led to both your deaths or capture." Damaris hisses that at me. "Now hush, please. I'm trying to listen. Fret in silence if you must fret at all, you two."

My teeth grind together, jaw jumping, but I'm grateful for the ping of anger at the paladin and her sharp comment because it gives me something to focus on that isn't the little thief I've grown rather fond of.

"Footsteps." Damaris again, snarled hastily. "Be ready."

There's no way it's the halfling, not on her silent, furry feet. That means Blossom failed. We lost our thief, down one when we could have used every body to fight off what is to come. And yet, I feel all the tension leave me as I switch into battle mode, welcoming the chance to fight, to act, to do something. My mind churns as I consider how best to get past Vosh just as Fleur's musical voice speaks.

"Wait. What is that?"

I strain to hear, hating being down here suddenly, needing to be up there with Damaris on the front line.

"Fighting. No, wait. Shouting. Something's wrong." Damaris hesitates and when she speaks again there's hope in her voice. "They're leaving. At speed. Be ready."

So Blossom came through for us after all? I send a silent thanks to her as I tense and, when air once again washes over me, this time in greater volume, I'm ready and moving the instant Vosh takes a violent step forward, forcing his massive body the rest of the way up and out the hatch overhead.

It takes him a moment to squeeze out but then it's empty and I'm the last up and through, leaping from the last step into the vast room on the other side, the hatch flipped closed as Graldor does the job while Damaris whips out her broadsword and stalks forward.

I run to catch her, spinning when I pull my own blade, the shield on my back now strapped to my arm, finally having the room I need to use it. Its weight comforts me as I examine the empty space, the giant hearths against both walls, massive iron pots bubbling over the flickering flames. Two vast tables lined with benches run the length of the room, tankards and food scattered over the surface, but the space itself is empty. Only then do I sniff and smell more smoke than I was expecting and realize dark mist drifts in from the doorway at the far end of the chamber.

"Fire." I run for the exit, the others on my heels, pausing at the half open doorway, the heavy wooden portal creaking when I peer around the corner. I can hear voices now, grunting and angry arguing, but no defined words. The corridor outside runs from side to side, more smoke gushing from the left, heading our way. The same direction the voices come from.

"Where are you going?" I spin to find Blossom standing in the middle of the table, a mug in one hand, a chunk of what looks like bread in the other. She's chewing, head cocked to one side, not an ounce of concern on her face. "The stairs are this way, dummy."

I hurry to her, helping myself to a quick bite as I pass, choking on the dry bread but swallowing anyway, a sip of a tankard enough to tell me the ale served the guards isn't fresh but it's wet and cool and helps wash down the chewy glue the bread's become.

We missed it, missed the curve of the staircase on the other side of the hatch in our haste to escape. I see it now, though, and gesture toward it, the others gathering food into their arms—Damaris sheathing her sword in favor of a few hasty gulps of sustenance—before Blossom is running gracefully down the table and leaping off the end, heading for the way up.

"Better hurry," she says brightly. "The distraction won't keep them for long."

"Do we want to know what you did?" I'm right behind her, glancing back, the rest of our group close behind. Grateful as I start to climb, counting places at the table, knowing we'd never have survived a battle against the hundred or so soldiers who the space could easily accommodate.

"Nothing too drastic," she says, while more smoke billows into the room. It's hard to ignore now, the cloud drifting toward us and heading for the stairs we climb. It's going to make going up difficult and I'm sure she didn't think of that but I'm not going to chastise her for saving us from death.

"Let me guess," Damaris growls. "You set fire to the place."

Blossom waves briefly at the smoke now gushing toward us. "Whoops. Guess I overestimated the flammability of their bedclothes. Shall we?"

"Before we choke on your cleverness," Graldor says.

We almost make it unseen. That would be too easy, wouldn't it? But, as Vosh grunts his way up this staircase, the main door to the room bangs open and two hulking orcs burst in. They don't see us at first, the thickening smoke dropping closer to the floor by the moment, but as I wait my turn, last again, I'm the first one to lock eyes with the bulky guards.

They freeze, shock on their ugly faces, pig snouts twitching, their deeply embedded eyes glittering black with lack of intelligence. But that only lasts a moment, the first who entered grunting something before bellowing out the door, its companion running toward me. It's a slow run at first, shambling and painful to watch, but by the time it's picked up speed halfway across the room it looks like a juggernaut of unstoppable fury bringing death toward me.

I level my sword, feeling my lips pull back, grinning in the face of the attack.

Memories be damned.

This. This is why I'm here.

CHAPTER THIRTY

THE ORC DOESN'T SLOW its charge as it approaches. Maybe it thinks it's invincible at full speed or doesn't register in its tiny brain the bright and shining blade in my hands is a risk to its safety. I'm sure it's accustomed to dealing with unarmed prisoners or even the smaller and less agile hobgoblins who we've already dispatched. Regardless the orc's train of thought, when it reaches me, it's huffing breath sounding like the bellows of a forge being pumped too hard, I'm fully prepared for the attack.

It's sadly simple, killing my opponent, though there's a moment when my sword slices through its neck the tip catches on the immensely dense bones of its vertebra and its forward motion drives it toward me. Blood spurts in a hot arc, splashing over my cheek and shoulder and slicking down the front of my shield while I jerk on my sword to free it from the orc. That twist in motion spins it sideways, its impact with the corner of the upward turn of the staircase so powerful I hear bones crunch. It collapses with a gurgling sigh, still bleeding, splattering my shoes when it strikes the ground. I dance back out of the way, heels of my boots impacting the first step as I spin and leap up after Vosh, now almost around the first turn.

"Sorry," he grunts. "Trying."

I push, though I know it won't help, but my adrenaline is high and I need to do something. Shoulder against his hip, I heave with all my strength while my gaze scans the doorway on the other side of the room, now awash with thickening smoke and making it impossible to see. But I can hear them, snarling and shouts and the clash of metal as they approach and I know despite my initial victory we're very rapidly running out of time.

"The staircase is defensible," I grunt as I shove against the giant troll. "I can hold them for a time. Tell Damaris they're coming." I cough then, the smoke at this level thick enough to make it hard to breathe and not getting any thinner.

"Up, now!" That was Blossom, her little voice shrill with command. Vosh heaves one last time and I almost fall as he escapes the tight turn. I catch myself and race after him, clattering the last three steps and out another hatch, gagging on smoke.

Hands grasp me, pull me free and something thuds, wood falling, the sound of Graldor growling magical words making hair stand up on my arms. And then we're in quiet, a small landing, with more stairs going up and a sealed hatch at our feet.

"It won't hold them for long," the wizard says, patting the wood and iron, the ring on the edge vibrating when someone hits it from below.

"They'll have a hard time getting through while their choking on smoke." Blossom grins, a line of soot across one cheek. "Not such a bad idea after all."

"Might I suggest the back patting wait for another time?" Damaris looks upward, leaning around the corner of the staircase. "It's clear for now, but we don't know if there's another way up or if the guards raised the alarm."

"And there's enough smoke heading to the tower we're bound to attract attention." It's cleared out already, but it only has one way to go. I cough out the last of what I inhaled and rise. "Let's go."

This staircase is at least not so narrow and Vosh has an easier time of it. When we pass through the next hatch, smoke pooling there and then escaping when I hit it with my shoulder—I refuse to go last this time—I blink into light and pause a moment to peek through the crack for location clues.

"Looks like the ground floor at last," Fleur whispers into my ear.

"Definitely." Blossom sounds far too chipper though it's infectious. Seeing daylight gives me a lift like nothing else.

"Carefully," I say, Damaris is already shoving past me, grimacing as blood transfers from me to her, before she's up and out into the light.

I follow, taking a moment to look out the narrow slits of windows, realizing we're far higher than I expected. "Second or even third floor," I whisper.

Blossom hops up, hands on the lip, pulling herself high enough to see before dropping to the floor again. "Second," she says, all business now. "This way."

"Wait." I grasp her shoulder, turn her around. We're in a small, round room, the hatch closed at our feet now, more stairs climbing upward. A narrow door stands on the far side of the space, away from the windows. Leading where? "We need a plan. So far we've just been barreling our way from one disaster to another. But if we're going to find the Soulblade we have to slow down and talk this out."

"Probably long overdue," Vosh says with a grin. "I'm thinking none of us really expected to make it this far."

From the grim and almost embarrassed expressions from the others, he's right.

"I'm climbing." Damaris is the only one who looks stubbornly dedicated to plowing ahead. "With or without you."

"So suddenly we're no longer useful, is that it, paladin?" Graldor shakes his head. "Fine, you run off then. We're going to do what we can to protect ourselves. Don't get killed, if you can help it."

She snarls at him but doesn't leave though she looks like she wants to. "Can we have this conversation on the move?" Damaris glances upward again, anxiety obvious. "We're sitting ducks here and you all know it."

"Fine," I say, pushing past her. "What do you want to do?" I slowly climb, though I wish I'd stopped to check the door below. I peer down and see Graldor whispering beside it, one hand on the wood, before he hurries to follow. At least one of us is thinking ahead.

"Climb to the tower, kill the Demon King and take the Soulblade back to my moth—" She stops herself before finishing, swallows audibly. "My queen," she finishes.

I stop moving, turning to look down at her, gone cold all over. "You can't be serious."

She doesn't meet my gaze, face tight and lips pulled into a thin, angry line. "I know it's rough," she says. "And direct. But we have no way of knowing what's up ahead and—"

"That's not what I'm talking about." I retreat a step, face in hers. "You were going to say mother, weren't you?"

Her jaw clenches, jumps while Fleur gasps behind her and Blossom lets out a low whistle.

"The crown princess didn't assign you this task," I say. "You are the crown princess."

Blossom giggles suddenly. "Damaris," she says. "Princess Amaris."

The paladin uncovered as royalty finally looks at me, eyes snapping frustration and fear. "So what? None of that matters now, Webb. My title, being heir to the throne, none of it. If the queen dies, I'm princess of nothing and nowhere."

"Truth," Vosh says softly. "However, it would have been nice to know who you are."

"Why?" Damaris turns to glare down at the others before spinning to return her furious gaze to me. "What does it matter? My sword arm is strong, my goals have always been clear. Correct?"

I shrug. "Even more now." I pause. "Your Highness."

She snorts, looks away. "Move it, Webb. My mother is running out of time and eventually we're going to run out of luck."

No arguing there. I'm not sure how I feel about her deception but knowing she's right about how little it matters in the grand scheme, I turn and climb again, trying to plan and knowing the best I can do is put one boot in front of the other.

CHAPTER THIRTY~ONE

A S WE CLIMB, WE pass more narrow windows, traveling up the now normal width and height spiraling staircase. Vosh still has to squeeze, but he's comfortable enough in the back I can focus on paying attention to the climb.

There's no further hatches, each level punctuated by another round room, another set of narrow slit windows. I take the chance to peek out each of them as we rise, shocked we haven't run into anyone yet, though Graldor's dedication to sealing the exits as we pass might have something to do with our continuing quiet ascension. Surely we can't continue unnoticed for much longer, but we've passed almost six floors so far without being challenged so my optimism wars with my utter faith we're going to be tossed into the fire pit any second now.

Curious to take a moment to glance out into the cloud filled sky, to observe the inner workings of the citadel and then out over the towering walls into the plains beyond. Orcs, hobgoblins and other foul creatures crawl the streets of the inner city, the stench of them a distant memory thanks to the breeze drifting through the windows. It's dark below, though it's full daylight, the tower we climb casting shadows over the cobbled ground far below, the roofs of the buildings black and dull as though the sun itself rejects the Demon King's citadel.

I see that Damaris's claim of her army massing isn't a false one, that shining soldiers have bivouacked in the distance with their tents and horses and glittering armor catching the low light that occasionally breaks through the cloud cover. I note she makes no effort to check on them herself and realize she's either feeling guilty for abandoning her people for this personal quest or is, more likely, too worried about her mother to care.

Now that I know she's really the princess of the realm, I look at her differently, though not disparaging in any way. How she carries herself, her confidence and poise, the fact I missed that regal nature, passed it off as arrogance. But it's not, I know that now. It's a lifetime of being raised to serve and to lead ingrained in her very bones and the plain, rugged lines of her face.

I feel for her future prince consort. He's in for a hell of a ride.

We clear the next set of stairs, the landing a bit bigger but nothing surprising. I'm about to suggest we stop for a quick check out the door before Graldor seals it when, to my shock, it opens inward, a tall and bulky orc entering with its head down and another at its back.

They're both in the small room before they spot us and freeze as I had, though Damaris is under no such stasis. She leaps past me, long, narrow dirk in one hand and a dagger torn from my belt on the way by in the other. She moves so fast, so fluidly, I'm gaping and just starting to shake free of my frozen state while she's already on the pair, dirk sliding cleanly through the lead orc's throat and the dagger finding the eye socket of the second a moment later.

They fall almost gracefully, her weapons retracted and the door shut smoothly behind them. She presses her back to it, not even out of breath, though two bright red points stand out on her cheekbones.

"Master wizard," she says, cold as ice, "I saw others coming. If you please?"

He joins her, retrieving one of the small items he'd stuffed into his clothing down below before the tentacles tried to eat us. There's stress in his tone though he manages to complete his spell in time, the glow from his hands and the short length of wood he's holding fading just as something hits the other side. We hold our collective breath, still and silent, as a guttural conversation carries out, muffled by thick wood. I don't speak orc, but I'm fairly certain someone's unhappy by this state of affairs and after a short attempt at pounding their way through, the grumpy monsters walk off, still arguing.

"It won't take them long to break through if they choose to put their backs into it," Graldor says, tension in every word. "This magic is untested, but I have enough to do a few more if necessary. I suggest we move on before Damaris's handiwork is discovered."

Our luck has just run out. I take the stairs two at a time, racing the paladin to the next floor, pausing to guard the door until Graldor joins us, puffing heavily. His face reddens, sweat dripping down his temples as he lets his hands drop and he meets my eyes.

"I think I've miscalculated," he says. "I can do one, maybe two more." There's an apology on his face. "And then I'm done in."

"I can assist," Vosh says. "Say the word, Graldor."

"Come on." Damaris looks flushed now, though I know she's not out of breath or even strained physically. It has to be her eagerness pushing her onward that speeds her heartrate and her breathing. I know how she feels, racing her upward once again, though this time, the moment my foot—in time with hers—touches the landing, the door to the citadel swings open and we're too late to stop it.

The space feels suddenly packed with bodies, four orcs and a handful of hobgoblins all scrambling to reach us. Were they lying in wait? I can only imagine they've been racing to catch us and finally have, the silence holding no longer as the orc in the back, one eye covered in a grotesque patch made of what looks like human skin, lifts a horn to his lips and blows.

I can't think about what that means right now. I'm locked in battle with a hobgoblin, quickly dispatched, though I realize I'm missing my dagger still. My shield is in the way, too bulky for the tight space, despite the fact it saves my life a moment before I choose to discard it, blocking the thrust of an orc short sword into my ribcage.

I cleave him from neck to sternum, the angle taking my blade from my hand, and I have to club the next attacker, a vicious little hobgoblin with teeth filed to jagged edges, using the edge of my shield. I hate to lose it, letting it go as I grasp for my fallen sword and jerk it free from the body of the thrashing orc. A crimson spray showers from the tip of my blade, casting off splatter over the wall and across two of his companions, while the sound of pounding feet out the door vibrates through the floor.

"More company!" I back toward the stairs, knowing there's nothing else to do but go up. "Get to the stairwell!"

Blossom slips around me, Fleur behind her, though the tall elf pauses to spike a hobgoblin through the top of his head with her slim sword before spinning in a perfect pirouette, decapitating another with a flick of her blade. She skips past me and Blossom, placing herself between the halfling and the next floor and I realize she's still in defense mode, not fleeing just yet.

"More coming down," she says in her song filled voice.

Of course there are.

"Go." Vosh grunts, one giant foot impacting the floor. It vibrates even more violently than under the approaching tread of the orcs. When he repeats the move with his other leg, I hear stone crack and fear he's going to shatter the rock under him and kill us all.

Instead, he reaches down and grasps the floor in both hands, pulling it up toward him as if he's turned it to cloth. The orcs and hobgoblins gape, while the rest of us do the same. Vosh meets my eyes, his glowing with deep red and I know he's reverting to his baser nature by choice.

"Webb," he rumbles. "Take them and go. Now!"

Damaris grasps for Graldor who tries to fight her off. But I shake my head at the dwarf while the sheet of moving rock solidifies between us and the orcs. Leaving Vosh on the other side.

"Run!" I spin to find Damaris already is, the other three with him, and turn to leap over the wall to the troll. But he's fighting, bashing orcs with his bare hands, tossing them like toys into each other and I realize I'm only in his way if I stay.

"Get out of here!" He bellows at me now, in full troll persona, seeming to swell upward and outward, gray skin taking on a darker hue. "I'll hold them!"

This time my arm doesn't vibrate, the embed giving me no guidance. I can't abandon him.

"*Do you choose to abort the scenario?*" That woman's voice again. No one else reacts to it. Am I the only one who hears her? "*Player WEBB-G. Abort or continue?*"

I grit my teeth against betrayal. "What happens if I abort?"

"*Reset,*" she says.

That means going back to the beginning. I can't do that. "Goal of scenario?"

"*Already defined by Player ONE. Acquire the Soulblade and slay the Demon King.*"

Wait, player who? My mind freezes in place. Player One is a myth—

"WEBB!" Vosh's deep voice has gone to grinding stone over stone. "RUN!"

"*Player WEBB-G.*" The voice pauses. "*Abort or continue?*"

I leave him then, heart pounding, feeling like a coward though I know this is the path I'm meant to take. The woman's voice falls silent, my actions speaking louder, I guess. But when I glance back, when I look down at the troll backed against a wall of his own making, tossing orcs and hobgoblins while they swarm him with numbers, I realize I don't want to do this anymore.

I just don't know how to stop.

CHAPTER THIRTY~TWO

I'M NOT EVEN AT the next landing and I run into the others fighting off a wave of hobgoblins. Blossom tosses herself backward into my arms and I catch her before she tumbles down the stairs, just barely.

"I have an idea," she says. "We have to get off the steps. They're just going to keep coming after us."

I watch Damaris cutting through the line of attackers at the top, knowing Blossom is right. Yes, the way is narrow enough she can keep them off of us for a time, but when she falls, it's only a matter of weariness and bad luck before we're taken out.

"What do you want to do?" I'm positive I'm going to hate the answer.

I'm right. "Climb," she says. Hesitates, looks sad as she peeks over the edge of the stairs and then leans back quickly. "I didn't want to say anything when Vosh was with us because, well."

He can't climb. "Climb what?" I look up but she shakes her head and points at the windows and suddenly I can't breathe and I'm shaking.

"You're crazy," I say. Try to say. While Fleur joins us, panting and splattered with blood, her bow tucked over her shoulder, unused in the close quarters.

"It's our only option," Blossom says. "Out the window and up as quickly as we can. Or find another way in. We're just asking for attack now."

"And we're not targets out there?" I wipe at sweat on my upper lip, startled when Graldor and Damaris skid down the stairs toward us.

"Just a few front runners to deal with," the paladin pants. "But there's more coming. What are we doing?"

Blossom reaches into her multitude of acquired clothes and pulls out a rope, a collapsed hook and shrugs. Before using me as a springboard, little feet pressing firmly into me as she throws herself at the nearest window a few feet away and slips through it sideways, waving on the other side. I inhale, can't exhale, reach for her when she seems to hover in midair a moment before the hook in her hand catches the stone lip and she falls, the rope snaking past my feet and out the window. And then she's in the opening, gesturing for us to follow, Fleur close on her back.

I hesitate, hearing the fighting below, the pounding of feet approaching from above. I'm surprised to find Graldor and Damaris are both still with me, staring at the opening in the window, none of us making a move. So I'm not the only one afraid of heights?

"We'll meet you up there!" I spin and run for the next landing, Damaris and Graldor on my heels. I slip in blood and on the spilled entrails of a hobgoblin, startling an orc on the way by as I skim past it when it runs into the room, Damaris dodging it just in time. I turn to defend, but Graldor is there, slamming the door shut behind the one lonely orc, his power flaring as he seals the way.

Damaris and I both strike at once, the orc falling in three pieces as her broadsword takes him at the waist and my blade removes his boar like head from his shoulders. He collapses, leaving us a clear view to Graldor and the panting, weary and determined wizard's clear decision written on his face.

"Go," he pants. "I can climb no more. And this door won't hold against them."

"What about the next one?" Damaris speaks before I can, surprising me.

"Reach the Demon King," Graldor says, "and it will be worth it." He pulls a small flask from his hip pouch and downs it, something amber flaring on his tongue. "Go, and hurry. Before I run out of power."

I've made this choice already, no easier the second time, spinning and racing up the steps with Damaris matching my stride. Her face is as grim as I know mine must be, and we thunder on, upward, past doorways still closed, no longer trying to be quiet or hide. Our only focus now is speed.

We're close, I can feel it, the windows slightly bigger now, the stairs more elaborate, carvings in the stone and the doors at each level etched and decorated with care. I don't know what we think we can accomplish with such a brash and headlong assault, but there's nothing else my weary mind can muster to try. I slide on a heavy dark carpet someone thought was a good idea, kicking it aside as Damaris dodges it, lunging past me for the stairs. Too late, both of us, this time, the doorway slamming open before we're even halfway across the circular room.

But we're not alone, the lead orc crashing to the floor with an arrow in his eye. I spin to find Blossom and Fleur in the window casing, the ranger already drawing another arrow. Her attack gives us the time to sprint the rest of the way to the stairs, the elf and halfling leaping inside and joining us on our flight.

My heart stutters when Fleur pauses at the halfway point and fires another arrow. Someone screams below and I know she's hit her mark.

Her eyes meet mine, faint smile on her lean face. "Fetch the Soulblade, there's a good boy." And then she's shooting again and I'm running, leaving yet another of my friends behind.

I scoop up Blossom who's weeping and limp, carrying her with me though I don't have the strength to do so for long. I'm panting now, legs on fire from the running climb, my body slick with sweat and the vague feeling of nausea growing in my gut. I can't keep up this pace much longer.

I almost run into Damaris's back, shocked to find she's stopped, stunned enough I set down the halfling only to have her turn and run back the way she came on swift feet, calling for Fleur.

I let her go. I have no other choice. Damaris looks down at me from the last step, a large door looming before her, wood dyed black and etched with what looks like golden runes.

"I guess it's just you and me in the end," she says while memory triggers and I see her differently, as someone I know. Don't I know her? But how and from where? Only then realizing she's in my mind in so many incarnations, in so many moments just like this one.

Different scenarios but history repeating.

Before I can ask her who she is, who I am, she inhales. And opens the door.

CHAPTER THIRTY~THREE

I'M EXPECTING AN ARMY on the other side. Instead, it's dark and quiet, almost fragrant with fresh air from being so elevated, I guess. Damaris raises one arm, sweeps aside a heavy curtain and steps out into light. I have no choice but to follow.

Well, not exactly true. I could stand here on the last step forever and wait for trouble to find me. Not much of an alternative.

She's tense, wary, though she seems much calmer than I'm feeling. I need to kill something, the drive to keep going more powerful than I expected. My embed shivers, making my arm ache a moment, while Damaris turns slowly and examines the room, exactly what I'm doing, until we're back to back in the middle of a large, round space filled with tapestries, the floor soft with black carpeting under our boots.

"There must be doors," I say in an oddly conversational tone. My voice sounds muffled to me, all the fabric on the walls and floor a shift from the stone we've been travelling through. Only the heavy chandelier lit with what seems to be a thousand wicks shows any sign of life in this place. The tapestries—varying scenes but all displaying some kind of battle between dragons and soldiers or giants against a castle or some other monstrous creature wreaking havoc—hang perfectly still and quiet, to the point I can't even remember which one we emerged from behind.

"Agreed," Damaris says in that same quiet, calm tone I used. "Split up or look together?"

The decision is made for us. The only warning we get we're about to have company is the sigh of air moving. Damaris and I lunge at the same time, heading for a shield of curtain, ducking behind it just as one of the hangings pushes aside and a small knot of orcs march through.

They pause in the middle of the room, snorting and snuffling and I wonder what they are doing. Their waiting makes me nervous, ratcheting up my anxiety as I clench my sword in my fist and fight off the urge to attack. Damaris meets my eyes, her own full of manic drive, but she shakes her head and I nod in answer.

Whatever or whomever they wait for, we seem to be in agreement. We'll wait, too.

Not for much longer. It seems like I barely have time to take a breath, the scent of old dye now in my awareness, faint dust raised by our disturbing this hiding place tickling my nose before another waft of air drifts past and a voice speaks.

"What news?" It's rasping and deep, modulated as if layered by power, making the goosebumps on my arms get goosebumps. I twitch at the sound, heart leaping to my throat,

Damaris flinching next to me, her lips narrowed into a tight line.

"We're still hunting two of the escaped prisoners," one of the orcs growls. His guttural tone is hard to make out and my brain fills in extra words to make up a full sentence. What I actually hear is, "We hunt two," or something similar. Funny what the mind will do.

"And the rest?" There's a crackling tone to the voice, like fire burns beneath his vocal chords. Definitely male and powerful, threatening.

"Still fighting." I almost exhale in relief, stop myself at the last second. At least the others are still alive.

"Deal with them." The voice sounds bored, annoyed. "The Soulblade must be protected at all costs."

"Master." I hear the tread of booted feet retreating and wait, still holding my breath, for the second waft of air that will tell me we're alone. It doesn't come. And when Damaris twitches next to me, I grasp her elbow ever so gently and meet her eyes. Beg her to wait with my gaze.

One second. Two. Three. Time stretches out into forever as my lungs beg me to breathe, to refresh the oxygen in my blood. Four. I almost release Damaris, almost give in to the demands of my body. Five.

Only then do I hear it. The faintest tread, walking away, feel the wash of fresh air and then nothing.

I pant out the stale breath in my lungs and inhale again while Damaris leans in and presses her forehead to mine.

"Well played," she whispers, the use of that word triggering the memory of the woman's voice, the ring of the bell, and again I have a thought. Player One. Impossible. Player One doesn't exist. But who is that, exactly and how am I so certain? Damaris obviously has no idea I'm thinking about something else, her focus, at least, where it needs to be. "Though we'll have to face the Demon King eventually."

I jerk back to the here and now. Then that was him after all. At least, she believes so, too, from the fear and determination in her eyes. I've been annoyed with her, frustrated, angry and even felt humor at her actions. But this is the first time I feel connected to Damaris and I'm grateful for the chance to call her friend. "Not without the Soulblade," I whisper back. "Let's go get it. And save your mother."

Her face crumples for just a moment, a mere flicker of what she's really feeling showing in her tired expression. So much sorrow, terror, guilt. How can she stand it? And then she's back to her usual self, all bluster and impatience and she's brushing past me and into the room beyond, leaving me to follow.

"This way." Damaris stalks across the carpet on silent feet, to the far end of the room and a towering tapestry with a massive demon dominating the center. Naturally. I almost snort at the obvious choice, but there's no time for amusement. The paladin lifts the edge of the curtain and slips behind it, holding it out for me to join her.

There's another staircase, this one plain and narrow but easily accessible for the two of us.

She unsheathes her broadsword, holding it out in front of her while I take the stairs sideways, keeping an eye on our backs.

I turn to look down when we're almost at the top, relieved to see we're still alone and am in process of returning my attention to Damaris when I hear her cry out. I spin, sword held low, to find she's disappearing from the last stair, hurtling forward as if jerked off her feet and through a half open doorway. I leap after her and freeze at the sound of steel striking steel.

A tall, slim woman with flames for eyes and smoke pouring from her lips swings a massive sword at the paladin, striking so hard Damaris is forced to one knee. She slides beneath the black blade of her demon attacker—she must be a demon and my heart pounds in fear at the sight of her—her own sword striking at the creature's legs.

They're already halfway across this new chamber, heading for the far window and a small balcony outside. I gather myself to join the fight when Damaris spins from the demon woman and meets my gaze.

"GO!" She ducks just in time as my lips part to warn her to do so, her instincts clearly well prepared. "Webb, get the Soulblade!"

I know better than to argue with her. I've already left everyone else behind for this sole purpose. And this fight is only going to alert the Demon King we're here, that we've made it this far. In fact, anything I do from this moment on is suicide. Because there's no way he's going to allow me anywhere near the Soulblade.

I turn and run for the only door in sight, knowing I go to my death but out of choices once again as my embed vibrates and glows white.

CHAPTER THIRTY~FOUR

THE DOOR LEADS ME to another set of stairs and I fly up them, feeling as if I'm possessed now myself. All of my focus is on reaching the top of the tower, reaching the Soulblade. My vision narrows to a tunnel before me, and when I burst from the next staircase and into the room above it, I don't even slow down as I register the pair of orcs that turn to face me.

Flames in their eyes. Burning smoke billowing from their tusked mouths. I hear myself cry out, a battle call, though it's as if that yell comes from a great distance. My sword moves at the end of my arm, an extension of myself, and while I know somewhere inside me, in a logical and assessing part of my mind everything that I do is practiced over and over again through many trials like this the bulk of me is here, now, in this instant and nowhere else.

The first orc charges like an enraged bull, head down, hands extended, but it's without a weapon aside from its possession and the claws and teeth nature gave it. My sword relieves it of one of its hands, whipping back with a hum as I quickly cut the air and then its throat, fire pouring out of its severed neck and cascading over its chest while it slowly collapses, the demon within it gushing out and howling at me before dissipating into a cloud of ash.

There's no respite, not when the second orc charges me through the remains of the first, bursting from the resulting smoke in a blaze of its own fire. And this one is armed, a short, wide axe in its large grasp, swinging out at my knees while I leap into the air and push back, both of my feet impacting its chest. I flip over, landing solidly on my toes, shocked—and yet not—at my own agility while my body keeps moving, completing the motion and using the momentum to drive my sword forward into its torso.

I have to duck the wild swing it aims at my head, twisting my blade deep inside it. Blood mixes with fire, gushing out of its gaping mouth, gurgling scream a fountain of flaming crimson. The burning fluid splashes my face, boiling hot. I flinch away, wiping at the scalding gush, feeling the embed in my arm twitch in response to the damage.

The orc goes down with a crash, but I'm no longer interested in it or its ending. The stairs it and its companion guarded call me upward.

One more flight. One more dash heavenward. I skid to a halt at the top, gulping air pouring through the huge, open windows, spinning on my heel, knowing I'm here at last. No more doors. No more steps.

Just a pedestal in the center of the room. And a giant, shining blade standing in the middle of it, as tall as I am. Hovering as if by magic, the tip barely resting against the stone, red wrapped pommel dark like blood, wound with gold, pommel stone winking at me.

I made it. Impossible but true and surreal and likely a trap. And yet, here it stands, waiting for me.

The Soulblade.

I'm moving again, my own sword clattering to the floor at my feet as I leap up onto the pedestal, four feet above the floor, my hands grasping instantly for the hilt of the magical blade. It's huge, bigger than I can carry, but I can't resist it. Victory so close, so real, a victory I've doubted despite this moment's seeming inevitability now. I can save my friends, save the queen, kill the Demon King. Blood singing with excited joy, I seize the prize and brace myself for its impossible weight.

My hands burn where they touch the leather, locking me to the hilt while my embed buzzes, turns red, and everything in me lurches toward the sword.

Someone laughs as I slowly collapse, though I can't let go, body draining of life and strength. My sleeve slides back, showing me the embed countdown, all of my stats retreating, slowly at first but gaining speed, HW dovetailing into the low double digits within seconds, the rest doing the same, pulsing crimson I realize with my slowing heartbeat.

"The Soulblade is well named." I know that voice, just heard it below. I manage to look up, through the growing dimness of my dying vision, to see a tall, handsome man, silver streaks in his dark hair, lean body clothed all in black leather, watching me with a smile on his face. Flames wake in his blue eyes, gout from his lips a moment before he reverts to human appearance.

The Demon King.

"What..." I manage that word. Lick my lips as I sag, body pressed to the blade now, unable to sustain my own weight but cleaved to the hilt without the ability to let go. "What's happening to me?"

"Why, it's taking your soul, of course." The Demon King circles the pedestal, arms crossed over his chest, sly smile on his lips. "You think I'd just leave it out here to be taken like this if it didn't have its own protections? It took the sacrifice of six of my demons, each carrying it in turn until they died and passed it on, to retrieve it and bring it to me." He sounds like that's more of an inconvenience than a sorrow. "Won't be long now, brave hero, before yours joins that of all the others who sought to take this blade for their own." He shrugs. "And those who have been damaged by it. Like the queen."

"You could have just killed her." Why didn't he?

"And miss the blade absorbing her soul?" He tsks at me, grinning fire. "A quick death would rob me of that pleasure. And besides, her suffering brings me joy. As does yours."

His voice fades out a moment and I blink, shake my head. I'm dying, close to death now. I can feel the last of my life oozing out of me and into the sword. Fool, idiot. What was I thinking?

"Now what?" I don't know why I ask that question of the air around me, but when she answers, I'm not surprised.

"*Soulblade scenario incomplete,*" the woman's voice says, as crisp and chipper as I remember. "*Reset or forfeit?*"

"I'm dying," I whisper.

"*Soulblade scenario incomplete.*" She falls silent again.

"Options?" I'm not dead yet, am I? "*Are you requesting a hint?*" She pauses a moment and something dings in the distance. "*Point tally permits it.*"

Something inside me roars no, never. "No hint," I whisper, though it's a stupid thing to do.

"*Understood. Soulblade scenario incomplete. Reset or forfeit?*" She's not insistent, though she keeps repeating herself.

It's only then I realize I'm still alive. That the Demon King stands frozen, still grinning at me, but a bird outside the window hovers, still and silent, and even the fire in the candles of the chandelier are immobile.

"*Game paused,*" she says. "*What is your command?*"

"No hint," I say. "But options?"

She doesn't say anything for a long moment. I hang there from the Soulblade, so close to death I can feel my heartbeat in obvious, painful contractions.

"*Options*," she says then, as if some choice has been made. "*Death or reset.*"

"Not reset," I say. "What will death get me?"

Again the pause, longer this time. I sigh heavily, aching all over. "Never mind."

"*Death is a hint*," she says then, suddenly. "*But a hint is not approved by PLAYER WEBB-G.*"

Death is a...

"Resume," I say, though I have no idea why I've said it, how I command this time and place. Doesn't matter, not anymore. As the Demon King comes back to life, the bird outside flapping once, the candles dancing into motion, I pivot my body sideways and lean into the Soulblade, knowing what I must do and how, that the slow and painful ending is the wrong way to go. That sacrifice, not cowardice, is the secret to the sword that kills me.

The Demon King roars in protest when he sees my intent, enough fear in his eyes flaring fire I know I've guessed correctly. But he's too late to stop me.

Death is a hint. The quick death he denied the queen, not her suffering he wished to prolong, but her salvation, perhaps? With my jaw clenched against the coming pain, I lean hard and cut my own throat.

Everything I am gushes into the Soulblade at once, the slow draw over. My life, my soul, my breath enters the metal. I feel myself absorbed by the steel, become one with the leather bound hilt, the core of me bursting into the gem at the apex, flaring into new life as the Soulblade's own spirit accepts and welcomes me and my sacrifice.

I feel him then, the maker, Borengald. Feel his hands in my hands, see though I have no eyes his gaze locked on mine. Smell the scent of the forge where the blade was made, touch the heat of it, feel the steam of water quenching its glowing red heart.

Courage and sacrifice from the soul of a true hero, his voice echoes around me. *Well come, brave soldier. I've been waiting for you since the day I was made.*

I've come to kill the Demon King, I say.

Then let us do as we both desire, he laughs in my head. *As I once sacrificed all I am to do. And never again shall a Demon King rise to threaten this world.*

Golden light spreads over me, his voice gone, but warmth and flaring energy filling me, swelling inside me and the sword and making me whole.

"*Level achieved*," her voice says as a bell dings softly three times. "*Soulblade scenario finale activated.*"

I blink and I'm alive and in one piece, neck intact, standing on the pedestal with the Soulblade in my hand. It's no longer a towering sword almost as long as I am tall but perfect for my grasp. The Demon King hurtles toward me, fire blazing in his eyes, pouring out of his mouth, but the Soulblade is faster, sweeping outward and taking him across the throat, severing his head from his body.

Blood spurts, arches through the air, a gout of it rising from the stump of his neck. Fire pours with it, a towering inferno of flame reaching for the ceiling, forming a swirling fireball near the chandelier. But it's attempted retreat fails, the flames sucked toward me, into the tip of the Soulblade and my arm vibrates from the embed and the power the weapon devours, as the Demon King's essence rushes into the prison of the Soulblade in my hand.

It's done before the head hits the floor, landing with a solid thunk on the stone, rolling toward the doorway and the stairs. Damaris leaps the last step and onto the flat, her foot impacting the Demon King's forehead, sending the ball-like remains spinning in a circle away from her. She gapes at it, at me, at the sword in my hands.

And laughs before running forward to embrace me, blood on her face, on her armor, but utter joy in her eyes.

"Webb," she says. "Well played."

Played. Player WEBB-G.

Player One...?

CHAPTER THIRTY-FIVE

IT'S NICE TO BE clean, to wear soft clothes and shake out my damp hair, to touch the healed skin of my cheek where the molten blood of the dying demon orc stripped the flesh from my face. And even more so to sit at a table with my friends and lift a tankard to salute them, all of them. Here, whole, smiling and with their own tales to tell.

The tent is muffled and quiet though the army outside sounds like they're readying for battle. Not so, not any longer. Thanks to us—to me, truth be told and accepted without flushing—they're simply packing up to go home.

Damaris sits with us, her face relaxed for the first time since I've met her, tall, lean body draped still in leather and a surcoat, no dresses for this princess.

She seems far more at ease with us than the endless line of soldiers and ranking commanders who've been bowing and scraping to Princess Amaris since we arrived in camp. The fact she made no small thing of our appearance, demanding assistance and guidance to the queen probably has no small part in the fact myself and our companions have had little issue with being challenged. If anything, I feel rather the hero and am trying my best not to let it get to my ego too much.

"Mother's taking care of the exodus," Damaris says, tipping her ale for a long drink. "Good of her, considering you saved her life."

I grin and salute her, savoring the cold, clean taste of the queen's own ale. My stomach gurgles around a few bites of a delicious meat pie I'm sampling between drinks, the scent of it making me want to bury my face in it instead of eating it a forkful at a time. "To the queen," I say.

"To the queen!" The others echo my sentiment as a young man in court livery, his pale cheeks barely fuzzed with the hint of a beard, refills my tankard before retreating to the edge of the carpet under our table. I have never been so grateful to sit and eat and drink and have nothing to do.

The last few hours are a blur, a happy blur, but wavering and indistinct none the less. Punctuated by a few cheery memories. Like racing down the steps with Damaris to find Fleur and Blossom about to be overrun by orcs, the Soulblade making short work of their attackers. The power inside it might be kind to those it deems worthy, but now that I've claimed it, it seems more than happy to devour the life source of its enemies.

To leaping the wall Vosh made and shattering it and his opposition while the failing troll smiled up at me.

To slamming through the door leading to the subterranean prison just in time to take out the legs of the hobgoblins leading Graldor, bleeding and unconscious, down to a new cage.

To the utter devastation of the Demon King's hoards as I cut the drawbridge chain with my new sword and let the army of Queen Vanarion inside to wipe up the mess.

And, finally, following Damaris to her mother's bedside, pressing the Soulblade against her wound and commanding the sword to release her spirit back into her body while the gathered courtiers and soldiers stared and whispered and Borengald spoke to me of all the magnificent tasks we have ahead of us.

All in the past, recent enough the memories still strike me if I let them linger. But I can feel myself stirring despite my happiness in sitting here, enjoying my victory. Something isn't over that has nothing to do with the mage in the sword and his suggestions of future endeavors.

I'm fairly certain I'm going to hear a familiar voice in a moment accompanied by the chime of a bell.

Instead of summoning that visit prematurely, I grin at Blossom, a faint feeling of desperation in my heart. Can't I just enjoy this for a while? It feels like things always end this way and I'm in too much haste to move on to enjoy the finale. That's what the voice called it, right? "You're still with us, my roguish friend."

"You doubted?" She tosses a soft roll at me. "If it wasn't for me, you all would be dead a million times over."

"If it wasn't for you," Graldor grumbles, also fully restored and looking resplendent in his new wizard robe, a bit of fresh silver now tracing through his thick beard, "we'd likely have come through this faster and without as much fuss." He strokes the length of hair at his chin as if proud of his new shining color addition.

Blossom sticks her tongue out at him while Fleur smiles indulgently.

"It has been my great honor to share this adventure with all of you." She nods to me, sips at her cup I know contains only fresh water.

"And you." I nod to her hand that cups the acorn of the eld oak Blossom rescued for her. "You're going home to plant that I take it?"

"I will find the grove from which it came," she says, "and return it to its mother."

"Dark elves await at the end of that journey," Vosh says, deep voice soft and yet not chiding or judging or even telling her not to go.

She nods. "Indeed. And yet, the tree calls for home and its needs outweigh my safety."

"Then you shall not go alone," the troll druid says.

Fleur looks away a moment, swallows, smiles when she meets his eyes, hers wet with moisture. "The way will be long and fraught with peril."

"What are we waiting for?" Graldor laughs then, slaps Fleur on the shoulder. The elf stares at him in surprise. "I'm in."

Blossom bounces in her chair, munching a roll with huge eyes. "Sign me up," she says.

They glance at Damaris who shrugs.

"I can't just leave," she says. Grins with a wry twist to her lips. "Maybe." Sighs. "We'll see." Laughs then. "Count me in. I'll figure something out and besides, you lot won't make it ten leagues without me."

Finally, all eyes turn to me. Something swells in my heart and I inhale to accept, to leap at the chance. They look like my yes is a given and it should be. It should. Just as a bell dings in my mind and she speaks.

"*Options*," the woman's voice says.

I look down at my embed, at the higher numbers, the healthy glow of white when it vibrates while the world around me freezes in place.

"List?" how do I know what to say? But I've been here before, many times. I feel it in my bones. My hand falls on the hilt of the Soulblade resting beside me as she speaks.

"*PLAYER WEBB-G, options are: A) Continue Soulblade stage as permanent selection, B) Start Over, or C) Select Next Stage.*"

So continuing here is an option. I like the sound of that, but not the permanent choice caveat. "What does option A) mean?"

"*Option A locks PLAYER WEBB-G. in Soulblade Stage until all stages are resolved.*"

My stomach tightens and as it did with the offer of a hint, my soul rejects the idea of remaining. It feels like quitting. Why is that? I can't abandon the others to finish what I started.

Wait, what others?

The other players.

I shake my head, wishing there is a way around these gaps in my memory that seem to know exactly what I need to do. And press on instead of fighting the loss. Option two is no option, I'm sure of it. I've completed what I came here to do.

There's really only one thing left. Select next stage. Whatever that means.

"I choose Option C." The words are out of my mouth before I can stop them and suddenly everyone is in motion again, though this time my new friends aren't looking at me with expectation. Their leaping to their feet, staring behind me. I don't have to look, to turn around, to know there's a doorway there of glowing white light. They're illuminated by it, falling back from it.

"I have to go," I say, standing. Leaving the Soulblade behind, the sword I was never meant to keep. I meet each of their gazes, trying to memorize their faces though I'm positive as soon as I step through that gateway—and it's a gateway, make no mistake—I'll forget them and my time here. "You have fun without me."

Damaris steps forward, extends a hand. It's only then I remember the tattoo on her arm and I gasp, fingering my own. She doesn't seem to notice, frowning at me.

"You're sure?" She hesitates, looks away, rubs at her temple with her fingers. She's like me, isn't she? Does she hear the voice, has she been offered options? Did she choose this stage, to stay? I don't judge her for that, I can feel the appeal of such a choice. Maybe I should stay with her after all?

But the pull of the gate calls, the lure to a new stage and I can't resist it now that the selection is made.

"You could come with me." I didn't mean to say that, either.

She shakes her head. "Not yet." She looks like she has no idea why she said that. "Yet? I'm sorry."

"I'll be seeing you." I'm sure of that. I wave, circling the chair I was once content to sit in, backing toward the growing light. It casts beams around me as I near it and I turn at last to look.

It's a hole in the world, a glowing white light that pulses when I come closer. My embed shudders one last time, falls still as I reach out to touch the edge of the glow.

Somewhere out there, maybe on the other side of this gate, are my memories, my real life, because this isn't. This is a game, some kind of scenario I've been enduring, and others like it. For how long? No way of knowing without finding out who I am. And I'm determined to do just that. While uncovering what this is all about and why I'm wrapped up in it.

Inhaling a shaking breath, anticipating an experience I feel in my bones but can't put details to, I step into the gate, pulled instantly forward and engulfed by the light.

CHAPTER THIRTY~SIX

WHITE LIGHT EATS ME whole, swallows me and takes me over, sucks me forward into a tunnel of brightness that is all at once familiar and terrifying. Blinded, I raise both hands to protect my eyes as I roll over in a ball, spinning sideways as if the light itself is a river or a gust of powerful wind, though I feel nothing from it.

I hurtle to an instant stop against something hard, though I know I'm not injured. I remember this! Only in bits and flares of thought, struggling to hold onto Damaris and Vosh, to Blossom and Graldor and the memory of the

Soulblade. Instead, as my mind fights to cling to scraps that fade faster than I can gather them to me, I hear a soft, female voice follow the musical ding of a bell.

"*Selection complete. New stage activated. Heartbite scenario commencing.*"

Wait, no, stop. I think I say that out loud, because rather than being flung off again—I remember this part clearly now, though I'm already wondering what a Vosh is and why the term blossom means something to me—I instead hear a repeat of the bell chime.

"*Scenario induction paused. State your query, PLAYER WEBB-G.*"

Did I do that? "I don't understand," I say. "Please, can you tell me where I am?"

"*PLAYER WEBB-G, Heartbite scenario loaded and ready.*"

"That doesn't make any sense," I say. "Heartbite?"

The voice must take the repeat of the word as a command. "*Confirmed. Heartbite scenario commencing. Good luck, PLAYER WEBB-G.*"

I try to cry out, to stop this from happening (again and again and again?) but I'm too late. My head spins, my mind aching but there's no more time to talk to the voice, no moment to uncover where I am, what's happening to me. I'm moving again before I can understand, comprehend, even draw a breath. The light whirls, sweeps across me like a river of rushing water, sends me diving forward, darkness appearing at the end of the glow, hurtling toward me too fast. My hands rise of their own accord, shielding me as I exit the light.

I'm on my knees, hands pressed to stone, faint moonlight shining in the towering window. I pant into the chill air, looking up in shock at sudden movement as someone rushes toward me, a flash of lace and velvet and pale, pale skin a moment before hands like cold stone grasp my arms and jerk me forward.

Fangs puncture my throat, my blood pumping out of me and into my attacker as I scream into the darkness—

AUTHOR NOTES

WHEN I WAS NINE years old, my father brought home Dungeons & Dragons and changed the course of my life forever. I know, that sounds dramatic, but I honestly believe without D&D as a catalyst, I wouldn't be the writer I am today. Listening to his deep, expressive voice guide us as our Dungeon Master, his storytelling all I needed for my imagination to come alive, he shaped my creative voice and led me down a road I'm so glad I followed, even if it meant I was a geeky nerdgirl who always felt a little out of place and totally awkward.

Fast forward to a short time ago. I have a passion for the books I write, the stories in my head, but I've been writing about teenagers and witches and post-apocalyptic illnesses. Horror chases through dark woods. Cozy mysteries. You name it, including one lonely romance novel.

Finding LitRPG was like coming home again, a chance to relive my days as first a human cleric named Ladaar and then as Dungeon Master myself when my father decided his time behind the screen was done. I haven't played in a long time, though I still have my dice, the original books, graph paper scrawled with maps and notes from campaigns I've hoarded all these years.

I hope you enjoy Webb's first stage. I certainly had fun writing it. I'm excited to take him on his next adventure, to see where his story takes him (yes, I already know how this series ends, eight books from now). As sad as I am to leave the traditional fantasy world of the Soulblade, there's so much more to explore.

Thank you for reading and happy gaming,

Best,

Patti Larsen

ABOUT THE AUTHOR

EVERYTHING YOU NEED TO know about me is in this one statement: I've wanted to be a writer since I was a little girl, and now I'm doing it. How cool is that, being able to follow your dream and make it reality? I've tried everything from university to college, graduating the second with a journalism diploma (I sucked at telling real stories), was in an all-girl improv troupe for five glorious years (if you've never tried it, I highly recommend making things up as you go along as often as possible). I've even been in a Celtic girl band (some of our stuff is on YouTube!) and was an independent film maker. My business partner and I are the proud co-creators of the Lovely Witches Club and webseries of the same name.

My life has been one creative thing after another—all leading me here, to writing books for a living.

Now with multiple series in happy publication, I live on beautiful and magical Prince Edward Island (I know you've heard of Anne of Green Gables) with my very patient husband and multitude of pets.

I love-love-love hearing from you! You can reach me (and I promise I'll message back) at patti@pattilarsen.com. And if you're eager for your next dose of Patti Larsen books (usually about one release a month) come join my mailing list! All the best up and coming, giveaways, contests and, of course, my observations on the world (aren't you just dying to know what I think about everything?) all in one place: http://smarturl.it/PattiLarsenEmail.

Last—but not least!—I hope you enjoyed what you read! Your happiness is my happiness. And I'd love to hear just what you thought. **A review** where you found this book would mean the world to me—**reviews feed writers** more than you will ever know. So, loved it (or not so much), **your honest review** would make my day. **Thank you!**